The Origami Bird

Elizabeth Ashworth was born in Buxton, Derbyshire, and grew up in north Wales, where she still lives, teaches, writes and paints. Her prize-winning poetry has appeared in a wide range of magazines in the UK and the USA. Her memoir, *So I Kissed her Little Sister* was published to critical acclaim in 1999. *The Origami Bird* is her first short story collection.

Also by Elizabeth Ashworth

So I Kissed her Little Sister

The Origami Bird

Elizabeth Ashworth

PARTHIAN

Parthian
The Old Surgery
Napier Street
Cardigan
SA43 1ED
www.parthianbooks.co.uk

First published in 2004
©Elizabeth Ashworth 2004
All Rights Reserved.

ISBN 1-902638-25-5

Edited by Gwen Davies

Typeset in Galliard

Printed and bound by Dinefwr Press, Llandybie

With Support from the Parthian Collective

Parthian is an independent publisher that works with the
support of the Welsh Books Council and the Arts Council of
Wales.

British Library Cataloguing in Publication Data.
A cataloguing record for this book is available from the British
Library.

Cover Design: Marian Delyth
from *Oasis* by Susan Lee

This book is sold subject to the condition that it shall not by
way of trade or otherwise be circulated without the publisher's
prior consent in any form of binding or cover other than that in
which it is published and without a similar condition including
this condition being imposed on the subsequent purchaser.

for Joyce and for Marnie

With thanks to Gwen Davies, Parthian Publishing Editor.

Go, litel bok
 Chaucer, *Troilus and Criseyde*

Stories

The Only Thing	1
Stone Circle	9
Vincent's Chair	14
Walking on Water	20
Who'd Want You?	28
Little Miss Mischief	34
The Origami Bird	39
The Armies of the Night	46
Tinsel	55
The Private View	62
The Siamese Tree	67
Writing to Jake Slinger	73
True Love Ways	77
The Net	84

THE ONLY THING

The only thing, her dad had said once to her, was art. And he was a famous writer, so he should have known. He had shown her how words could be used in ways that altered or clarified the meaning of a sentence; taught her how an idea could captivate the mind of a whole generation.

Renate had believed him, without thinking about it and without question, even when things had got a bit weird with them all. She looked again at the family portrait on the cover of the book Leonie had written, observing the shining-faced child she herself had been, and saw the sureness and gratitude of being loved. It had been taken in the living-room of the house in France, on the first Christmas after buying it. Her dad, Lemuel, glancing bashfully out, was holding his wife's hand awkwardly, lifting it a little as a childless man might, in an attempt at playfulness, and his other arm was hanging in its tweed sleeve, in a silly, futile way, by his side. The living room suggested itself already, two months after the purchase, as being at the hub of a hectic social whirl, amid solid appurtenances of wealth: cards and invitations were crammed busily and abstractedly on the mahogany mantelpiece; decanters and glasses stood upon the carved table, and a half-demolished cake crumbled merrily upon its silver salver; there was a sense of society, of breezy comings and goings; of the realization of an ideal. The photograph had been taken in front of an enormous tree: behind Lem were looped thick swathes of tinsel, and baubles – the kind with a mirrored interior, surrounded by a little red frill of Christmas cheer, which flashed shards of superficial icy light back into the camera, as glittering and insistent as though it were yesterday.

Marta, her mother, who had wanted to be a dancer, held her hand in the photograph, at arm's length. She had given up her ambition by then, and was letting herself go. The comfortable-looking extra wadding was accentuated by the thin belt of her velvet dress, that lay not around her waist but just across the broadening hips, above the beginning of the pleat of the skirt, now stretched open to allow the swinging leg to emerge in its shiny nylon stocking, and its four-inch heel. The right heel almost touched the sock of the child — herself, Renate, who, in turn, emulating her mother and father, swung her own small leg at a smaller angle.

So there they were, in a row: Lem Biermann and his family, making a rather stiff, pristine tableau, but kicking out in unison; a synchronised step into the New Year, against the over-loaded tree, the stylish art nouveau lamps, the dangling baubles, the shelves of books, and the blurred, untrodden French countryside beyond the window.

Renate studied the blurb of the book, pausing at its description of her parents' "mythic romance", reading how, tragically, from its starry beginning, when Marta had been a creative prodigy and Lem a literary prince, the relationship had so swiftly degenerated, to resentment, envy, bitterness, slanging matches, estrangement and madness. An ancient, private fund of speech bubbles floated "Queer boy" and "Manipulative bitch" over the heads of the matronly flapper and the smiling novelist — insults that she had, once, later, actually heard them shrieking at each other. And above her own head, that of the shining-haired child, with her lank ribbon, her dumpling legs and patent leather shoes, the plump bare arms and reserved gaze — with a jolt, the bubble of "Nevermore".

Sighing, she leaned across for her handbag at the edge of the sofa, where she had been eating her supper while reading the heavy biography, and took out her mirror again, to see which of her parents she resembled more closely.

She was old now, she knew: the grey-white curly hair was brushed up from her brow in her own odd flyaway style, but there was, still, the keen, intense spark of Lem's eyes, and the need to laugh of Marta's lips, behind the frosty veneer she presented to the world these days. Her heart quailed, and the impudent thought darted into her head again. If only they could have done it! If they could have had the love *and* the art! But, most of all – daringly – if they could both simply have been glad that they were the mother and father of Renate.

But being artists, and art, of course – changing the world – that was the only thing! She, who had come to merely exist at the edge of their turbulent lives, had always accepted that fact. It had been the rationale behind all her work in television, before the bosses had seen her off – the silver quiff and the refusal to wear make-up by then no longer the trademark of independence and strength, but merely embarrassing proof of quirkiness and stubbornness. So now she sat at home a lot, like this, eating in front of the television, getting heavier, occasionally playing back her interviews, smiling at the pointedness of her questions to politicians, rather missing the job that she'd had because of the Biermann name, but well-pleased with her fearless on-screen self.

She rose to wash the plate she had just eaten from: strands of beansprouts were already browning at the edge; the water she had failed to drain off completely from the tin puddling nauseously with the cooling oil from her stir-fry. She grunted, surprised at how much of an effort it was to lurch from the sofa, but happy that she was no longer required to cook for others, jealous of her privacy and freedoms. Renate had grown to revel in her independence and strength, and to exercise an easy scorn in the arena of relationships.

The Only Thing

She was expecting a visit from her friend, Hella: the only person she felt she could really talk to, and to whom she could let things show, if only a tiny bit, through the cracks in the façade. Hella was what people described as "solid gold" and "all heart", meaning she exhibited (and maybe felt) compassion, and didn't make judgements.

"I never really have had convictions, as such, because I'm always open to the other side of things, you know, and there are two sides to everything, and everyone has a point of view."

This characteristic was a fortunate one for her husband, whom, despite his womanising, Hella insisted on describing only in terms of his charisma. Slim and fashionable still, Hella persevered as a popular and conventional editor, self-deprecating and emotionally articulate in the most accessible and modern manner. Sometimes, Renate had suspected that this warm and embracing nature might have another aspect: it might mask a fear of being alone, or of being condemned by more powerful others. Hella, smiling and nodding softly and kindly, would be forever urging the speaker onwards to more exposures, in such a damned everlastingly understanding way! And then Renate would laugh to herself, because she felt that she herself was so truthful and uncompromising, in comparison; though she had been turfed out of her job, and her daughter's life, she was proud not to be muddied by that same desperate need to be liked or loved.

It had been a very long time since she'd seen Leonie, who, to everyone's delight in the arts' world, was both a writer and a dancer. Except that Leonie, also in that world's opinion, was a bit mad and an attention-seeker, and didn't speak to Renate these days. Everyone had forgotten what had been the reasons for the fallings-out, but they were nevertheless sustained.

Hella was at the door, now, with flowers and gin, sweeping freshness and hope into the room, smelling of something unobtrusive but flowery: the picture of the mature, yet girlish, professional. She frowned at the greasy smell of cooking and the scene of crumpled newspapers and cushions as she picked up the book.

"So here it is at last! What do you feel about it?" Hella was flicking through the pages, dwelling on early pictures of Renate at boarding school, and the mother and father arriving in England on an "ocean-going liner", wrapped in furs (Marta) and double-breasted tweed suit (Lem).

"She makes much of Dad's struggles and successes – quite rightly – and Mother's complexities and difficulties. She's very proud of them, and obviously finds me a bit of an irrelevance. I get a mention as a hack."

"It's just her perception, you know, Renate," Hella cooed, automatically, throwing her coat down. "It's good that she has taken all this trouble, and is serious about her family's achievements."

"Theirs, not mine."

"Theirs is the story to sell the book, not yours."

"Theirs is the artists' life, you mean. Art being the only thing."

"Yes, art is important, of course, and artists' lives, and that's why people are interested in the Biermanns – they've become iconic, and they're glamorous to us, because of the compelling desire to express themselves artistically, and because they lived such a fast, creative, self-destructive life." The friends were making themselves comfortable, with drinks and followings to the kitchen and toppings up with ice and lemon. "Don't you find it interesting that all those events and escapades have been brought together like this – that Leonie has made art herself, out of all those messy family adventures!"

"Yes. It's a real coup."

Renate was smiling to herself, staring down at the pages, at an excerpt from one of her father's letters to her mother. "Renate will have to stay at school in Livorno at least until the summer – we'll find the money…" and remembering the quadrangles and corridors and matrons and intermittent cool and heat, and the waiting with her bags at stations, term after term, for strangers to collect and deposit her.

And here was a picture of Lem and Marta with a controversial artist, and, automatically, Renate pointed as usual to the framed drawing on the wall, reproduced in the book, and Hella exclaimed at the wonder of it all, jumping up obediently to examine it.

"That will go to Leonie, I suppose, after me."

Her baby Leonie, who became the ebullient girl and the accusing young wife, who told Renate that she had failed, as a woman and a mother, that she was flawed, neurotic, unable to give; that no wonder her husband had walked out on her; that she, Leonie, would never have kids, in order to stop the rot now.

Renate leaned back against the tapestry cushions, and Hella saw how she was ageing and adrift, without work and without family.

"She's bought into the fantasy. The day she said those terrible things to me, I left her house and went into town, and as I walked the streets, I passed a child in a parked car, looking right at me, through the window. I thought for a moment that she might be wishing I were her mother, as I used to with women who passed me in Italy, and France, and Spain."

"You wanted a different mother from Marta Biermann?" Renate looked at her, and past her, at the bookshelves with ever more volumes: *The Short Stories of Lem Biermann*; *The Example of Isadora* and *Living Dancing* by Marta Biermann; *The Essential Biermanns*. "But it was such a privileged life! To study in Italy! To meet painters and sculptors, and all those other celebrities! To be the only child of those two, at such a time! It was a golden age, Renate! What a passport to life it has been for you, surely!"

Renate looked at the family portrait again, imagining Marta's warm hand, recalling how the photographer had asked them to swing their legs out: "Now, sir, madam, Miss Biermann, too, please!" The bough of the Christmas tree, soft against the back of her sash, was buoying her up into the movement required of her; she sensed the almost-touch of her mother's fashionable shoe, and knew without looking how the nylon clung smoothly and sheerly to that beloved shin. She had wanted to stop the world; to keep her mother and father hand in hand with each other and with herself in a bright chain of flesh and blood and love; she had longed to stretch that free, child's arm, bare in its party frock, to a future of her own, with a husband, and a home full of cards and cake and Christmas, and a child like herself, whom she would call Leonie, she had decided, as the shutter had closed.

"I remember when that picture was taken, Hella. It was the day my dad said it: 'Art is the only thing.'"

Hella was nodding, all attention, but heavy-lidded.

"He was right, of course. It is."

Renate was back, vividly, in a cold bedroom, looking out across snow somewhere in Italy, just before Christmas. Her friends were packing to leave, collecting cards and presents from their lockers, and kissing her goodbye, or inviting her for New Year. She had lain the tissue-wrapped famous drawing carefully on top of her trunk, covering it with an angora jumper, having first examined it carefully, for the thousandth time, as her friends' voices had rung down the chilly passages. It was a rare landscape sketch, in pencil, with rough, solid shapes of rocks in the foreground, and the cypress groves and squat villas that she recognised from her own trips to that faraway French countryside. She had held it in her trembling hands, for a minute or two, trying to feel succoured by it, too proud to cry and say she wanted her mother and father, not able to recognise that truth, while the twilight had deepened, and the friends had grown fewer, and a clock had chimed deeply and lusciously and cruelly in the empty flagged hall.

That morning a letter had come from her dad, to tell her that her mother was ill, and must go for treatment to a London clinic. He would be on a reading tour of England until May: would she mind staying where she was over the holiday – he was arranging for some friends of theirs to collect her, and Italian Christmases were such special fun. She would be taken to shows in Florence, and meet some extraordinary creative people: writers, painters, dancers, musicians, theatre folk from the Negro revues. It would be a whirlwind holiday – didn't she love the gaiety of those marvellous singers in their red and yellow spotted blouses, and their harlequin suits? Her mother, he had been sure, sent all her love, and so had he, of course.

Renate closed the book softly and looked at her sleeping companion, staying late, she knew, to make her husband wonder where she might be. She thought of that Italian Christmas, the swiftly-packaged books of impromptu gifts for her, the quarrels the drunken people in brilliant costumes had in the kitchen, and the strange cold bed she was put in, among snowy mountains she couldn't name, that had looked like heaps of unwanted ice-cream in the moonlight.

STONE CIRCLE

You didn't know whether to just accept them as they were, or try to analyse them. There was a book about them, but it was too technical – full of the diameter in feet and inches, then metres, in brackets, and bits of irrelevant anecdote. Such as a couple of the cairns covering a giant's bones, or "sacred land", which was later proved not to be, and so on. But one had caught my attention – a story about a woman turned to stone that was supposed to bleed if a piece got broken off it.

That night, we'd had a meal, me and Rob and his new wife, and he'd called a taxi for me. In the dark, as he had shut the door after shouting goodnight, I must have slipped on the steps – they're big and uneven, and overgrown. It wasn't until the next morning, in bed, that I realised I'd hurt myself: the sheet was rubbing against my sore elbow. I put my fingers there, to feel the seeping graze, then peered over at it. It was then I remembered the steepness of the steps in the night, with some pale yellow poppies just glimmering at the edges. Recalling it again, I was more acutely aware of the rough-cut stones, the soil and the foliage: it seemed now as though the journey had been arduous in some odd way; as if my legs and feet had been leaden.

"You were probably pissed," my flatmate said, when I showed him the red scar. I had drunk wine, yes: that would be it, and yet the feeling of having waded down into a kind of sea that pulled against me remained in my mind, like a dream-sequence.

It had been my day off, and Rob and Jess had invited me to go with them to see some early Neolithic sites – stone circles, mostly. We'd spent the day as the guidebook advised, complete with stout boots, overtrousers, a compass and the OS map, which always made me feel middle-aged and frumpy, but then we were all getting on a bit, and these things were useful in themselves. But I'd had an idea of scrambling about, just as I was, in my pumps and old trousers, like we had done when we were kids, without any of this getting ready and always having sets of clobber in the boot.

Of course, we got lost. We always did, trailing round and round the lanes with Jess giving little exasperated sighs when we came across the same layby we'd passed twenty minutes earlier. But there was no actual fight between them: they seemed able to manage their small irritations, which I found enviable – I've a low frustration threshold, apparently. I sat in the back of the car, with the atlases and the flask and the Polos, and I watched the changing light of the afternoon, feeling more peaceful as we passed by stone walls, with their white lichens bleaching into shapes of flowers and galaxies, and their foxgloves in delicate tones of violet and pink sprouting from high banks.

We found what Rob thought must be the place, and parked, then went through the ritual with the outfits, looking for possible rain, hiding purses and God knows what – the usual rigmarole. It reminded me of trips I used to make to the beach with a windsurfer boyfriend: he'd spend hours fastening his board to the roofrack, then driving miles to the coast and back again, so he could have a small spurt of carefree sport, if the wind were in the right direction. All seemed contrary to me, as I strolled behind Rob and Jess to the site: a perverse importance placed on things.

The path wound ahead: the two figures, in layers of anoraks and windcheaters half-turning to keep me included, as we passed through grassy lanes of marsh flags, yellow like the poppies, flimsypetalled flowers, which would fade in a few days, but were splendid now, in gold plumes along our way. I thought of Edward Thomas's poem: "Old Man" – something about an avenue, nameless, without end....

Rob would be sixty this year, and I wasn't too far behind, incredible as this fact was to me. He was no longer a child, leaping across fields and beaches, at one with the flotsam of the tideline – picking up razor shells, and the flat, rubbery, ochre-coloured weeds. Could this leathery-skinned and bespectacled retired civil servant, with his grey short-back-and-sides, his pedometer, his Rennies and his bumbag really be the boy who had shouted, "Charge!" at my friends from school, and poured tomato sauce down his shirt to feign death in our back porch, and told me that Barry would never go out with me because I was too fat, and my breath smelled of eggs?

Soon, Rob had disappeared, and Jess and I chatted as we continued forth. Then I became more aware of his absence, and called to him, immediately imagining that disaster had befallen him, as I would when he would vanish like this when I was small. My heart thumped, but I showed no fretfulness, and waited for his inevitable reappearance in the field beyond. We pressed on through the thicker grass, round a corner, and there he was.

He was at the stone circle, labouring over the guide book, when we caught up with him. He looked up without speaking, preoccupied in some way.

"What are they *for*, though – ?" I'd just started to say, but Jess was standing in the centre already, her arms flailing.

"Feel it! Feel that energy!" she commanded. We joined her, but I experienced only a sense of sky, high wind, birdsong and silent landscapes, like that of childhood. Rob sat down heavily at the base of the stones, and fished for his camera. I read the inscription on an upright, wooden heritage frame-thing.

"How do they *know*, though?"

"You can *feel* it – this was where they brought the sacrifices, alright," said Jess.

Rob had set the camera on the grass, and now scurried to join us. We stood saying, "cheese" on a slab at the spot, where according to the book a young girl had been cremated. It was hard for me to imagine these things, and to pay homage, because whatever had happened, and we could never know for sure (well, I couldn't), it was to people just like us, with the same emotions, desires and blood. There was always the possibility of the truth being misrepresented, and to me that diminished these so-called facts of history. I didn't like history, because of that – and the way people from the past become heroic and events accrue power merely because they happened in another time. Yes, it was marvellous that other human beings may have stood on this grass, but what difference was there between those people of thousands of years ago, and those of yesterday? Wasn't it only the same phenomenon that separated Rob of the sixty-year-old skin from the ten-year-old, in his jeans from the market? How was time so *distinguishing*? I decided, as I leaned on the stones, it was a leveller at most, but essentially a distractor and deluder.

"I like to think about these stones in the downpours of the ages, in the drizzles and winds and sleet and storms, with the light changing, and the cloud shadows falling across them," Rob was saying.

A week later, I showed the photo to Sid, over a cup of tea, with one hand up my sleeve, locating the scab that had formed over the graze on my elbow.

"Nice shapes – very sculptural, aren't they? What are they – Neolithic? Aren't they supposed to go as far down into the earth as they stand up? So that's about four or five feet both ways."

"Oh, I don't know. They're just stones, aren't they?" I said.

Sid smiled. "We'll never know the truth about them, I suppose, except that they're not there by accident."

"Maybe they are – glacial or something."

"No, they've been placed there on purpose. They had a function. They meant something. People believed in them. It's important, because it places us – links us to the past – and gives us a sense of belonging, and continuity."

I looked at the three of us, in the photo, and pictured Rob in a den we'd made when we were kids. It would be raining, and inside would be leafy and dark and damp, with muddy copies of the *Beano* torn up to make a fire, and meat-paste sandwiches and pop. I would go out into the wood for a pee, and watch it steaming up from the leaf mould around my sandals, smelling its hot yellow scent as it streamed out of me.

"I suppose so."

I felt the scab float away into my palm, a perfect sliver.

VINCENT'S CHAIR

Ultimately, Vincent had written to Theo, the sight of the picture should soothe the mind. While encouraging her with her painting, before he had died, Jimmy had shown Miranda the room at Arles. "He'd suddenly understood the power of pure colour. You should try it – just splash the paint on. Don't worry about the drawing too much – and I know they're very subtle and restrained and all that, but forget those tentative watercolours of yours for a bit. Let yourself go. See the picture *glow*."

Miranda was on her way back from the town where they had grown up: she had gone to look for the seat in the bowling green where Jimmy, suddenly an old man, looking silly in a charity shop body warmer, which he should never have needed, had spent his last summer.

She walked up the road from the station, her feet aching where she imagined she might have fallen arches: she was sure she could feel her sandals against the skin on the soles of her feet. It came as a small surprise to her, as any new description of yourself, such as tiring easily, and wanting an early night does: it identifies you as being just like the rest, like other people; it is a shock in an outrageous, yet oddly comforting way.

She'd only been away for one night, but it was enough for Miranda to look at the pavements beneath her flat feet with fresh eyes, as she always did, when she came back from somewhere. Usually it was from a trip to London, or from seeing a friend further afield, and the deeper the enjoyment or engagement with each experience of another, in another place – or, in this case, the keener the sense of loss of her old friend – the more sudden the revelation of the truth of her existence here.

Miranda had looked out of the window as the train drew in, standing now on the side of the sea, then watching the hills. She decided that what she liked about this place was just that: the ocean and the hills, and, apart from that, nothing. Circumstances had brought her here, and, she'd always said, here was as good a place as anywhere. It was as good as London, where she might go to an exhibition at the National Gallery, and it was as good as Cumbria, where she'd seen Dove Cottage, and the actual couch where the image of the daffodils had flashed upon Wordsworth's inward eye. And it was as good as Cricieth, where she'd stayed overnight and painted a smudgy picture from the windows of the B&B, in watercolours in the early morning rain. She'd hung about with some arty types in the evening but hadn't managed to say anything about what she felt about painting, and had gone early to bed.

Jimmy had not been able to go to art school, because of the illness which had struck him down at eighteen, but had raved about Vincent all his life. She had taken him the book of prints to hospital, when things had started to deteriorate. "His art is *passionate* – above life and death, Miranda. Can you imagine him in the cornfields, in the blazing sun, 'cheerful as a cricket', as he wrote to his brother? Complete bloody menace. Poor old bugger."

"I don't think I would have liked him much, myself," she had answered, slightly alarmed, as always, by the idea of breaking boundaries, only able to do it while latched to Jimmy's coat-tails, as it were.

"This chair in The Potato Eaters is almost exactly the same as the one in the bedroom at Arles, you know," he had observed, leafing through the book, both of them ignoring the catheter tube and the pathetic little locker and the easy-clean vinyl flooring. "His personality just shines through! So it all comes right in the end, if you stick to your guns."

She walked on, past the little shop that sold plants and wooden and metal mobiles, the butcher, with his insistent notices abut his BSE-clear meat, the estate agent's on the corner, to the crossroads, where she pressed the button and hoped the gang of lads opposite would disperse before she got there. Continuing along to her house, Miranda tried to imagine she had never seen this road before, in the way Jimmy had advised her: it was full of cottages, with flowers in pots in the small front spaces, or, like her own, set back along long paths. She looked at the dying roses among the fresher blooms on a briar twined round her gate, and pulled off a handful of petals absent-mindedly. The curtains were still drawn: it was odd to see them closed in the summer light, as if someone were ill and didn't want to see anybody. The bowl of cat biscuits was almost empty; the window cleaner's money was still in its envelope in the place in the wall where milk was once delivered, now painted in turquoise emulsion paint, and filled with stones she'd sprayed silver and gold, which looked dully precious in the right light. Miranda stepped into the side garden, and found some tiny, perfect alpine strawberries under their leaves. She gathered seven or eight and ate them all at once outside, pulled up some thin weeds that came out easily, aware of the red, yellow and purple shrubs between the branches of a flowering cherry, which already bore some small, blackish fruit.

Inside it was cool and quiet. She pulled the curtains back roughly, and kicked off her sandals. On the table in the new light lay a little pile of petals, from two previous occasions: the latest red and yellow cluster, drying and friable, and now the fresh, pale pink, most recent scattering.

She had caught the evening train the day before, and got off an hour later at the other end, to walk along the prom. Taking the familiar dusty path through the park to the bowling green, she had rambled across places she'd known for over twenty years, some of which were now overgrown and vandalised, but which had narrowly kept their essential character. The occurrence of bushes and wild flowers had been the same as it had always been along these routes: the scents and air at certain times of year unmistakable. When they were children, they had spent most of the summer in the park here, wandering into the green occasionally to watch the old men and hear the clack of the bowls and the ripples of applause in the sunshine. A neatly-clipped hedge surrounded the bowling green, and there were two or three entrances leading in from different parts of the park. You walked down a gentle concrete slope and then you were on the bordering path where the bowlers' wives sat, and other old men, in the sun, on the seats which commemorated others. It had always been sleepy and smelled green and as if it had been full of fat bees, and the men themselves had ambled and droned and cruised over the shorn camber in their twill slacks like old moths.

Jimmy had seemed very much out of place there in his last days, but, as he said, it was better to be in the open air, with a bit of company. He couldn't draw or paint any more, although he'd always been the best at art, and used to sit on the kerb on the way home from school to show Miranda how to exaggerate people's features in caricature. He had read poems to her, too, having memorised the long swathes of Tennyson or Longfellow that the headmaster had admired. She remembered his blond hair and his khaki shorts, which set off his tanned complexion so delicately. One night they had eaten beech nuts, at his suggestion, of course – she could see the same tree across the park where they had grovelled about like piglets, picking slender, shining red-brown slivers from peculiar, heart-shaped dried husks, whose edges folded crustily away. Another time he had persuaded her to help him turn all the taps on in the bowling green toilets and bang the doors closed, and then run off, Jimmy yelping with glee. They had been pals, though he had laughed at her puppy-fat and her slowness in learning.

As she recalled the gleaming, white-spotted jack, coming to rest softly in the sandy channel at the edge of the grass, a voice had come from behind her. "Excuse me! How on earth did you get in here?" Miranda had found the first gate locked, then managed to let herself into the green by merely lifting the latch of the second. She hadn't been here since Jimmy had died and then, in the following weeks, with some old school friends, she'd donated a seat in his memory, with a shining brass plaque.

The woman, in her blue catalogue twinset, spoke with a fussy Lancashire accent: she had obviously retired here, and clearly represented the bowling green committee.

"I just opened the gate."

"It should be locked, by rights – we've had no end of vandalism. Kids made a fire on the green last year!"

"Where's my friend's seat?"

A plaque caught the sun at the other side of the green, but it looked too new, and as she approached she did not expect to find Jimmy's name. The other seats looked dilapidated, with planks missing and varnish peeling, battered and weather-beaten. A breeze blew the fragrance of mayblossom across the hedge, and in her mind she was ten again, with a satin hairband and a new best dress.

"We've taken the best seats into the pavilion because of the damage that was being done to them," the woman was saying, backing off. "You could ring the secretary, Mr Hillman. I haven't got his number, though."

"I'll find it."

The woman had allowed her to pass, and Miranda took the path across to the patch where they used to look for four-leaved clover, then back-tracked across a rough, stony trail, overhung with elder. A mix of impressions from years ago mingled in her mind with these green and white scents.

"He was an artist; that was the important thing, and he was an influence. We're all an influence in others' lives, so it hasn't been wasted. Whatever you are, whoever you've been, lives on."

He was never going to reach middle age, the doctors had said: some thought it was a pity he had been here all his life, and never studied properly, or married and had children.

Miranda had stayed over, and had woken to the sound of seagulls, and the sounds of lorries delivering to the supermarket. She liked the cries of the birds, and the sensation of being near the sea, on the coast. Later she walked the mile back to the station for the train home.

****

Miranda fished out her telephone directory to look up Mr Hillman's number: she'd complain to him about the seat's absence, and how much it had cost, and how it was the only memorial they had to Jimmy. On her table lay the book of van Gogh prints that she had brought back from the hospital, with Jimmy's sketch book and paints. She opened the book, and looked at Vincent's chair, and thought of the enthusiasm with which he had gone to Arles, and his fallings-out with Gauguin, and his sad loves.

She read a fragment from the text above the painting: *...this room became the focus of all van Gogh's dreams.*

Then Miranda put the directory back, pushed back the curtains further to let in all the sunshine, and, leaving no jagged edges, carefully tore out the print from the book. Its colour vibrated hotly, and the picture seemed to writhe in her hands in the still room in the shimmering brilliance of the afternoon. She would paste it up, she thought, in Jimmy's honour, there in the middle of her clean, white living room wall. In time, of course, she would have to frame it. The edges were beginning to curl a little, even now.

WALKING ON WATER

Uncle Bert nodded as his wife passed him a plate. Fay watched as he began to tuck in to sliced beef, gravy, carrots and mashed potatoes. A small jar of mustard, a blue-rimmed bowl of tinned peaches in syrup and a can of evaporated milk stood further away on the worn cotton tablecloth.

"You want dinner?"

Auntie Sheila asked this, without thinking, every day, and every day Fay laughed and said yes, please, and Sheila would then set down a smaller version of Bert's for Fay, and take her own later. This was now an established ritual that would be impossible to question, either jokingly or in earnest. Fay knew that there was no intention of making her feel unwelcome: she understood that this was the way Sheila had been brought up, like her own mum. You had to get the dinner on the table for the breadwinner – the man – and then the women ate what was left. It was a tradition, like donkey-stoning the yellow front step, and scrubbing the lino floor for Christmas, after pulling up all the rugs and carpets, taking them outside to hang on the washing line, and banging them with the yardbrush. Sheila was proud of her cooking and cleanliness and proud of her front step and proud of Bert.

It hadn't been easy, getting used to each other, but it was five years now since Fay had been taken in to live with them. Her mother and father had died within two weeks of one another, in an Asian flu epidemic. Childless Sheila, her mother's younger sister, lived with Bert five houses down, so it was considered that the transfer wouldn't be too devastating. Fay would attend the same school, and have the same friends, and the same chances in life as if she had been with her own parents, Sheila had vowed, wiping her eyes with her hanky after the funeral.

Bert sat in silence; his eyes fixed on the middle distance, as ever, when he was eating. Fay, a plump nine-year-old now, watched him cut delicately into the meat, pat the gravy into the potato, munch it all at deliberate length, and swallow in a strangled gulp. The knife and fork were then laid together on the empty plate, which was pushed to one side, and the bowl of fruit pulled mechanically to the fore. Then Bert would pour the evaporated milk from the tin's jagged V-shaped hole, where Sheila had stabbed it with the tin-opener, and spoon up his pudding, without a word.

After dinner, on weekdays, Fay would return to afternoon school, Sheila would wash up and have her nap, and Bert would get back to the shop in the village. Fay walked the same route to school every day, up the alley that passed the back yard of her old home: sometimes stretching up to peep over the irregular slats of the fence to see how the grass had grown over the border of their little plot, and sometimes crying a little with forced tears. She couldn't really remember much about her parents now and while enchanted by the idea of being a changeling or misplaced princess, sensed vaguely that she had experienced loss. Then she would hop along, on and off the tree-lined pavement on the road to school, caught up in ideas of the story she was writing, or the book she would finish that evening.

Sheila and Bert were doing their heroic best, everyone agreed: Sheila even made Fay's clothes, and Bert let her help in the shop at the weekend. They had tea together at five o'clock, while listening to the wireless, did jigsaws and played Snap! or Newmarket, which Bert taught her, and at nine every night, Sheila or Bert brought her a glass of milk, and tucked her in.

Fay came to the corner where she turned for school, opposite the shop where Uncle Bert was manager. The sign glinted in the sun: Shipton's Family Grocer's. Fay loved every curl of every fat gilt letter, with its hint of grandeur and taste, and on Saturdays would hurry along to help fill the blue pound bags of sugar, or brush out the back room, where rice and flour and salt and all the other dry goods were stored. Sometimes Bert let her hand over to a customer the three-quarters of boiled ham in its smooth greaseproof wrapper. The slender sheaf of lean and fat lay heavily in her hand, imbued with glamour: she could visualise a scarlet tomato and a lettuce leaf flanking it upon a willow-patterned plate, as the news came on the wireless at five o'clock, and bread was being buttered, and steaming tea poured into the milk of a matching cup. Fay imagined much, and read much – randomly dipping into the *Reader's Digest* and the *National Geographic*, and the set of encyclopaedias that Bert was paying for week by week. Bert was very keen on information, Sheila had told Fay, rolling her eyes in jaded acknowledgement of her husband's keen intellect. To Fay, Uncle Bert was the fount of all knowledge: he used an arcane, adult vocabulary, and phrases that fascinated her. "It's a very *singular* thing," he would say about something unusual, or, about a woman recently widowed: "That poor woman, living in *viduity*."

As they walked home, companionably, he told her stories from his three favourite books – *King Solomon's Mines* and *Lorna Doone*, and *Moonfleet*, which he read over and over, and solemnly decreed to be classics. Sometimes people would come round to the house to ask for Bert's help in filling in a form, or in writing a letter to the council, and he would bring out his Parker fountain pen and the lined notepaper, while Sheila set the table with a pot of tea, a home-made malt loaf and scones.

"You're a right little blue-stocking, I *don't* think!" he once laughed, after showing her the sepia pictures of African women, when Fay had blurted something about an extinct tribe. She hadn't understood if this were a compliment or an insult, and hadn't dared to ask what "blue-stocking" meant. But he had seemed pleased that she liked the red-bound books, and would sit on the sofa in the evening sometimes, smelling of brisket and cheese, and point at hydro-electric power schemes, or sequoias in Canada. One picture, in a *National Geographic*, had always held Fay's attention. A child was standing, in a place where there was a war, Bert had said: a little girl in a man's jacket in the sand, holding out a cigarette packet to the passing troops, as if to plead asylum or understanding. The child had no mother or father; it was alone in the world, in the desert, in someone else's clothes, depending for survival on the whim of powerful adults, surrounded by scattered stones that threw long shadows in the remorseless light.

In the shop, Fay watched Bert wipe with a damp dishcloth the insistent traces of bright pink bacon from the edge of the gleaming slicer, then she mooched about reading the labels of coffee jars and biscuit tins, and practised spelling piccalilli, or doing multiplications in her notebook. Bert once told her, as he stood with his swatter in wait for a fly that buzzed in the streaming sunshine, that he had been interested in study, when he was a boy, but hadn't been able to go to college because he had needed to earn a living, there and then.

"I always liked languages. And science. I'd have studied Latin, if I could. Been a doctor, maybe," he said to Fay, and she thought that he would have made a good one, with his pale, woman's hands, washing everything down with Dettol and bleach at the end of the day. "But that's not for the likes of us hoi-polloi, by the look of it."

"Is that Latin, Bert?"

"Greek. It pays to increase your word-power."

Fay had seen pictures in the family album – Bert as a baby, lying on a tartan blanket, then Bert in rompers, then suddenly a young man in long pants, and slicked-back hair, standing with his grandpa and some other old men outside the Legion, then in the sombre wedding photograph, with Sheila on his arm. There had been no middle part to his life, he admitted, surprisingly, as he locked the shop up: it was as though he had gone to school one day and then got married to Sheila the next. "And I'll be stuck here for the duration, I expect. Ad infinitum."

Bert managed things well at the grocer's, but Fay had noticed the way he addressed the customers, which she would mimic for Sheila back at home, and have her in stitches: "'Thank you, Mrs Sharpe, ever so much! Very much obliged, dear! Are you sure that's everything now – how about a taste of this delicious fresh brawn?' And you can see he hates them all really and wishes they would choke on it!"

With her friends, Fay went on nature trails, poking sticks into everything, to see what it was made of, gathering spawn in jars, and writing up the details in her notebook. Bert read it one night, and she found it in the morning, to her annoyance: her pages of careful diagrams stained with grease from buttery fingers. Then he had got fed up with the jars on the draining board, and thrown them away, telling Fay that the tadpoles had turned into frogs and hopped off into the night. Fay, ignoring this pathetic attempt to cover up the deed, decided she didn't care. There were still ladybirds to fish from nettles, like spots of blood, and raindrops turning to diamonds in the waxy nasturtium leaves, the silver balls splinting and fragmenting like mercury. In delight, making connections and cross-references, she experimented and recorded and processed information, while Sheila continued to cook and clean, and to shop for the best apples and cauliflowers, and Bert's responses in the shop became ever more coldly oleaginous.

Mrs Urquhart, her English teacher, believed that Fay was

something of a prodigy: she was to be the lead in the school play, and had won a writing prize. Fay had run home to tell Sheila, breathlessly explaining the plot of the story, that she had based on the picture of the abandoned child, in the magazine. "That's lovely, Fay! Aren't you clever!" Everyone believed she would do well: she had overcome her bereavement; she was confident, popular and bright, and the world was her oyster. In her pinafore skirt, made of grey flannel from Bert's old trousers, and her gaping cotton socks, Fay shone in the debates and the speaking aloud competitions, and Sheila boasted about her still to the neighbours, feeding off her prowess like some dainty scavenging bird.

These days Bert ate his meals in silence still, and left the table quickly, telling Fay to lend Sheila a hand, and to stop messing about with pencil-cases.

"No, no, lovie, you get on with your homework – that's far more important," said her aunt, reverentially, cheerily stacking up the plates and cups. But Sheila didn't ask Fay about the work, in the same way she hadn't wanted to understand the theme of the story: it existed merely as a talisman, or a key that would let Fay run free, in a terrifying, unsignposted way. Sheila knew only the worn runes of her mother and her grandmother, that predicted fulfilment in sacrifice; gratification in service. So Fay helped a little, while disdaining the repetitive chores, and stopped going to the shop on Saturdays.

Bert had taken to reading pigeon-fancying magazines, and doing the football pools round, and didn't much seem to want to sit and read with her any more. When her end-of-term report came, he told her to watch out that she didn't get too big for her boots. That day, at dinner, as though hypnotised, Fay tremblingly passed her last roast potato to his plate.

One hot afternoon, a week or two before the scholarship exam, Mrs Urquhart set a spelling test on the blackboard. The first word she asked the class to spell was "yacht". Fay was the first to walk out with a piece of chalk, to scrawl the word "yaught".

"No... o," smiled the motherly woman, confident still of her pet pupil. A few attempts more followed, others now stretching up for "yatch" and "yautch". Fay asked for the chalk again, and the usual expectant hush fell. She strolled to the board, and drew down from each corner the dusty white legs of "Y", following it with a wobbly, but huge "O", and a triumphant "T". The teacher looked crestfallen. Fay was puzzled: she had remembered some complicated consonants for a second, then decided it was a trick. She knew she was a good speller: she was aware also that Mrs Urquhart had faith in her, and was now embarrassed and humiliated on her behalf. There had always been a joyful bond between them: a respect for one another's worth – Fay's innocence and eager genius; her teacher's wisdom and stature – and suddenly it was awry. While revelling in her gift, suddenly clouded by the desire to belong, Fay had made a stupid mistake. She felt dismay, and glancing at the windowsill, as she went back to her desk, flushed more deeply. The strawberry ice lolly she had placed there at registration and forgotten had steadily melted on its stick: now there was just a small nub in a great, brilliant pool of crimson.

Fay sat at her desk in the sunshine, and sweated in her pinstripe skirt, whose waistband and braces restricted her roughly. When she thought about it, away from the crisis of the moment, of course, she knew perfectly well how to spell "yacht". But something had disturbed her reckoning: her power had dissolved, even though she had seemed so blithe and almost to walk on water.

Fay walked back home at the end of the day in the setting sun, past the grocer's shop with its gilded letters, past the fence that was once her only horizon. She had decided to re-write the prizewinning story about the girl in the picture who wanted to give a present to the soldiers – there were things she could see that she needed to change.

But she wouldn't tell Auntie Sheila, who, when she got in, was making fairycakes, with white frosting and a little red cherry on the top. And when Uncle Bert came, at bedtime, to tuck her up, and sit unsmiling in the dark, she wouldn't tell him, either.

WHO'D WANT YOU?

That's what Pete had said to her, this morning, when she was getting dressed. Cathy had sat at his feet, crying. He'd taken her face in his hands and said that she'd be ruining two lives, if she left him, and also that she looked careworn.

"Who would want you?" he'd said, staring at the face he'd once professed to love every pore of.

She was glad to be out of the house, and on her way to work. She'd taken to saying things such as the only place she felt happy these days was in a supermarket.

On the way into the building, she passed this naughty kid, with ginger hair and crooked teeth, who was often stationed there, by a window, on a chair at the top of the stairs.

"Hello, Miss. Are you our now-and-again teacher?"

"Hello, Denny. Are you our now-and-again pupil?"

He chuckled enthusiastically at this, as he was always being kept in, or running off.

Cathy sat in the staffroom, while teachers came and went. One mentioned that Denny seemed unhappy today.

"He came in early to get ready to go on the science trip, but we're not allowing it."

"They're a horrible lot," someone else said, of Denny's family.

The science teacher was arriving, with a good-looking stranger. She was wearing walking boots, trousers of some strong fabric, and a fleece – likewise the young man. Cathy had seen them drive up to school behind her – the girl had revved a lot, before swinging neatly into her usual space.

In the staff lavatory, Cathy was told that the man was her boyfriend – a student.

"I thought she looked bouncy," Cathy said.

"No wonder," said the woman.

The young teacher was already famous for her discipline, even though she'd only been at the school a year. Organising trips, getting letters off to parents, bringing boyfriends in – there was no end to her confidence. Some of the kids hated her, because she screamed at them, but the books on her desk were always in perfect sequence; her marking was bang up-to-date; worksheets and textbooks were numbered; the location of every pencil was on record. She was thorough, efficient, energetic: a good teacher.

By now the boyfriend had been arranged among the others, and was shyly drinking coffee, while the girl checked the notice board for details of the field trip she had organised. Cathy watched her running her fingers through her tangled curls, loosening her fringe, talking busily and loudly, bright-eyed, panting and sweating slightly. The lists seemed to be in order.

"Hope the kids'll be good for you," said Cathy.

"They will be – they're my form," the young teacher said.

Cathy knew that Denny – when he attended – was in her form, and she had seen, yesterday, on the lab desk, the plans for today: the draft letter to the parents, which said that the children would be collecting specimens, and samples, and "small animals from the river". Denny would have enjoyed that, she thought. She remembered the sensation from childhood, that river smell of weeds and brownness, and poking about with a stick, in ponds and streams, in wellies, finding things like water boatmen, or nothing, but slithering about on makeshift stepping stones, bent importantly and analytically on the stirring of the gravel bed.

Now she, too, regarded the noticeboard. She was down to invigilate an exam in a familiar classroom: that was a perfect start to the day, because she could look across the kids, through the window and out at the grassy bank and sky, and think. All she had to do was to keep an eye on them, for a hand going up, for a tissue or a fresh sheet of paper, or to listen out for a dropped pen that she would tiptoe over to pick up, and graciously place in front of the child with whom she normally had a monumental feud, and they would smile softly and benignly at each other, both buoyed up by the sense, and the relief, of power lying elsewhere for the time being. On her way to the exam, Cathy passed Denny, and asked him if he minded not being allowed on the trip. Denny shook his head. His eyes were red.

"I've got to stay here all day," he said to Cathy. "That's my class – they're all going." Children were lining up excitedly at the bottom of the stairs. The science teacher passed them, on the way down, punching the air with her fist on seeing Denny. "Yes!"

This exclamation, expressed with glee and confidence, and not an iota of self-doubt, caused the two at the top to glance at one another again.

"I'm never coming back to this school," Denny said to Cathy.

In the exam room, Cathy established herself at her seat, with the school's mobile phone before her and her bag neatly at her feet. The starting and finishing times had been written up on the whiteboard by a senior teacher, and his instructions for the use of the phone were incomprehensibly displayed on the desk. Cathy just hoped she wouldn't have to use it. She'd stick her head out of the door and try and grab a passing person, in an emergency, because she didn't know if the moulded, sticking-up part was an aerial or just the shape of the phone, and she would no doubt place the wrong bit to her ear, and the kids would laugh, and it wasn't a risk she could take, if someone were passing out or having a fit or being sick or starting a period.

Ahead of her, through the window, the bank looked green and pleasant. There were four panes of glass, and through one she saw a bird, which then hopped to be contained in the next frame, where it pulled a worm out. She noticed the bird's long tail, and then heard the sound of humming, as the big school mower grew close. Cathy quietly left her seat and moved to the window, where, just in time, she managed to gesticulate to the groundsman to be quiet. He mouthed "Oh, sorry!" and cheerily circled away, and the sound grew dim.

In the restored quiet, Cathy moved back to her place, where she sat looking at the bowed heads, feeling safe and protected by the organisation, in the way she did in the supermarket, and thinking at last of what Pete had said.

She was a little bit shocked, she realised: things had somehow reversed, and now he was the one in charge. She'd discovered he'd been unfaithful, and threatened to leave him. She had never felt cherished, exactly, but had blindly believed that Pete was her soulmate. He'd said she was "too good to be true", to one of her friends, at first, and she hadn't really understood what he meant by this. She suspected that it was the sort of phrase a person would use who wasn't very good himself. But she'd fallen in love with him, partly because he seemed so sure about it all. Then they'd got married, but really because Cathy had wanted to. She'd thought they ought to make that lifetime pledge to one another, and she'd imagined setting up home, and going to auction rooms, and so on, and this had given her a feeling of woman-and-wifeliness. He'd spent his money on other things, though, and they'd been poor. That's why she'd trained to be a teacher. On their wedding day, Pete didn't seem very happy, or to think that he was the luckiest man in the world to have her – this was a romantic phrase she'd been struck by recently, hearing it spoken, mundanely enough, by a person in something like *EastEnders*. It never seemed that Pete thought being married was anything special: he still had a private life, and things she wasn't given access to. Yet in the beginning, he had been obsessed by her. As soon as she had responded, the fire had gone out, and now she was "careworn", and he was a philanderer. She couldn't work out how it had turned out like this, or what she should do. Every day, she had to try thinking about it, as if it were all someone else's problem: she had really meant it when she said that thing about the supermarket. How could someone who was supposed to love you grow tired of you so quickly? How could he betray you? How could you abuse the goodness that was too good to be true? Cathy couldn't grasp the smallest element of what was happening to her: her thoughts came dully, and she was in a daze.

Who would want you?

Then suddenly, she sat up. I'll show him, she thought: I bloody well *will* leave him, and I'll make a new life for myself, and put him behind me, where he belongs. The bird had now moved to the next pane; the exam was over.

She dismissed the children, and stood with the papers in her hand. She put them all in order, according to each candidate's number, then checked them over and over, before placing them safely in the box in which they had to be delivered to the school office, with the mobile phone, and the instructions for its use, on top. She wanted to seem as inside-her-own-skin and as capable as the science teacher. She then set off for the main part of the school. At the top of the stairs, Denny still sat. The school day had ended, and the trip was over. There was the usual rush and tumult of bags and bodies and shouts and disturbed air, making suddenly absurd his crime and his penance. In a few moments the building was empty of pupils and staff.

Cathy decided to have just one last word, because, she thought, here was someone worse off than herself: she, at least, was an adult with some degree of control over the miseries of existence. She would work out her problem with Pete in her own mind, and never feel this bad again: she felt, tremulously, that she could start to let go, to rebuild her life. His opinion of her would no longer matter. She addressed Denny in the silence with a new warmth and enthusiasm, flushed with her decision. Denny, too, could get up now and go home, and tomorrow would also be a new day for him. Beneath them, as in a film, they could both see teachers hurrying out with briefcases, hats and winter gloves, and children thronging in gangs and intimate groups, bags hanging from shoulders, mud covering legs, new letters stuffed into pockets.

"Did Miss say anything when they got back, Denny?"

Denny didn't move or answer, but shook his sandy head, again and again, like someone grieving, his thumb perilously near his mouth, his widened gaze fixed somewhere she couldn't discern, between the corridor, the car park, and the laughter.

LITTLE MISS MISCHIEF

Harry, Millie's husband, was wanting his wife to take him back, after a brief affair. "It's not that I blame him for going," Millie had said, looking at Bet through tears, her eyes reddened and her skin blotchy and roughened. "You've got to see it from his point of view. I mean, if I were a man I might want someone younger and prettier. It's nature. I don't know what to do now, though. How can things ever be the same again?"

Her best friend Bet, in the process of stowing away a pile of her son Aaron's books and comics for charity, had hugged her and said that she'd been right to throw Harry out. "Let him cool his heels for a while, and then decide what *you* want."

Once, Millie had been going to teach Aaron to read. She remembered the delight with which he'd first understood the word "daisy". They'd been sitting on Bet's sofa, with Aaron's finger trailing indifferently across words in an alphabet book – he'd been about three – when she'd seen how the shape and sequence of the letters had suddenly jumped out at him. She had watched, holding her breath, as he'd pointed to where it occurred on the opposite page: "Dazy! Dazy!" His light brown hair had smelled like grass, and she'd nuzzled her nose into it, laughing at him, so full of promise, and so much at the mercy of life. She'd told Bet then that she'd help him with his reading. But not very many opportunities had presented themselves, and now Aaron was nearly thirteen, and spoke to Millie only when strictly necessary. He would mooch past in town, with his friends, and grunt at her from under his close-fitting bandana.

"He's growing up, that's all!" Millie said to Bet, glad to see that Aaron didn't feel that he owed her anything; that, despite her having been his mum's friend for years now, he could choose to let go, without a fuss. She'd been hearing things, lately, though, which she'd refused to relay to his mother – that Aaron was involved with a gang of lads who'd vandalised some dustbins, by putting lit paper inside. He was just doing what his friends did, she decided privately: just as she herself had done when she was a kid. Millie had told Aaron vague anecdotes from her childhood, and then hoped afterwards, ruefully, in conversation, that she hadn't been a bad influence on him. She didn't, in her heart of hearts, think so. She'd told him about how, in primary school, they used to play with plasticine, which turned grey from all the handling, so that all the original reds, yellows, blues and greens had marbled and then run into each other, and you couldn't tell one piece from another any more.

"We called it 'clay' in those days. The teacher used to keep it in old golden syrup tins. I loved modelling, and we didn't have any clay in our house, and I was dying for some of my own. So one afternoon, when we were tidying away, I hid one of the tins in my knickers – we used to have these baggy knickers with long legs with elastic round the hem – and took it home."

Aaron had giggled, eating Marmite sandwiches in Bet's kitchen, looking up lightly from his comic, which was full of the violent, crudely-drawn scenes Bet frowned at. Millie had embarked on more stories: "Little Miss Mischief, I was known as – always up to some prank or another! We had these very wide window-ledges in our bedroom, and after my mother had tucked us up one night, I climbed out of bed and hid on one behind the long curtain. When she looked in again she thought I wasn't there and she was frantic!"

The image of her mother's stricken face and the tormented tears of relief was perplexingly sharp, so she moved on quickly: "And then there was the time I painted this girl's plaits –"

"Where's my sweet little baby gone, Millie? One minute he's doing Mother's Day cards and the next he can't bear me near him."

"He's a good lad, Bet," Millie shrugged, entranced still by old copies of Beatrix Potter, or Rupert Bear.

"No, he's different. When you realise, it's too late. I hear he's been hanging about with lads round the telephone boxes, and people are scared. He denies it, of course. I'll speak to his teacher."

Bet was irritated at Millie's blind defence of Aaron. After tea, when her friend had gone, Bet lifted her son's graffiti-covered school bag from the kitchen floor and shook out the battered exercise books. Within the pages of *English: Poetry*, she read, copied out in inky, *faux*-copperplate, adolescent handwriting:

Of man's first disobedience, and the fruit
Of that forbidden tree whose mortal taste
Brought death into the world.
           From *Paradise Lost* by J Milton, Esquire

She looked up as he shouted something about seeing her later, the front gate slammed, and Aaron disappeared into the late afternoon.

****

It had been three months now: the two women were wandering through Millie's garden.

"He's going to miss this in flower," Millie murmured, catching a leaf from the lavatera between her fingers, and shooing off the cat that was about to scratch up her newly dug-in pansies. "And the roses – we've got all sorts: yellow fragrant, climbing pink and some lovely old-fashioned reds. I don't understand how someone can plant things, and then just abandon them."

Last summer Bet had sat with Harry and Millie on the front step of the house, sharing a beer as the sun went down across the lawnful of daisies, and the grass grew dark under the hedge. Now Bet pictured Harry, smiling and panting under sacks of loam, staggering up the garden path; digging with his wife in the sun's heat; planning where new borders and fruit trees would be. Harry might have been a deceiver, Bet reflected, but at least he'd been able to admit it, and beg forgiveness. She admired him, in a way: that day in the garden she had watched him lean on his spade, sweating, pleased with himself, wholly absorbed in the task at hand, like a child. Bet knew that Millie still asked herself at what point had Harry been able to leave her, and then want to return, and realised that it was not vanity that made her friend wonder, but an insuperable dilemma: how and when did love become not-love, then love again?

Picking up her shopping bag and purse, and pulling on a thick cardigan, Millie made her way down the hill to the village in the cool autumn sunshine. Outside the greengrocer's, she noticed cars weaving their way gingerly around a broken bottle. A group of lads, including Aaron, all wearing the same kind of oversized jeans and jackets, was huddling together and laughing in the shop doorway.

"This isn't funny, boys – will you kindly pick up that glass?" Millie asked the youths, hoping that Aaron would not feel singled out. She returned home with her shopping, taking a path through a park, past a tree to which kids had tied a thick rope to swing from. Aaron and his friends now skulked about there, kicking at bits of branch. The tree overhung a bank strafed of all plant life and littered with broken twigs, fresh soil and dying oak leaves: the crisp packets and tin cans that had accumulated at the bottom of the slope mixed in depressingly with dirt. Where the lads had been swinging out over the path, a fence leaned, flattened and useless. Aaron, holding the rope and about to take off, called hello, but just as Millie smiled happily back she saw collusion pass swiftly through the group. One minute Aaron swung past her: the next she was suddenly thumped in the back by the trainer that flew off his foot. Millie hurried homeward, her face on fire. She could feel a bruise beginning under her cardigan, but couldn't bear to investigate.

That night, the cat's yowling was plangent, broad and full, with a salacious note that un-nerved her. When she opened the door, he sat there, impassively, his eyes glazed and unseeing. Harry's rockery, with its trails of misty white arabis and purple aubretia in the gloaming had become a flurry of indefinable colours and shapes.

Millie bent towards the animal, but he ducked her reach before slinking swiftly into the house to crouch tensely in a corner, trapping with mouth and paw a trembling mouse.

"Out! Out!" she shooed, and scooped up the dying victim in a dustpan, before chucking it randomly over the flower beds outside.

The whole preposterous thing branded itself in her mind: the cat's instinct to trifle, the mouse's to flee, the scent of the evening, the open door, and the swift body soaring sightless over blue forget-me-nots, lying like paper stars in a green night.

THE ORIGAMI BIRD

The display was in the foyer at school as you walked along towards the headmaster's office. It was getting a bit dog-eared, because it had been up for a while now, ever since the Japanese girl had been there, on an exchange, or whatever it was. The drawings were in ink, on sheets of white paper, pasted onto grey-brown sugar paper, and at first had been very impressive. You were struck by the attention to detail – the kind of thing you'd never get in this country, with that old-fashioned pleasure in play that you feel the Orientals still must have. "Let's Make a Crane!" it trilled. And there, in about seventeen drawings, was how to do it.

Every morning, Fran walked past and tried to read it, without stopping. She didn't want people to think she was actually interested in origami. She wasn't. What she was interested in was the feeling of purity and delight she got from the diagrams: the innocent hope that bending a plain piece of paper this way and that could yield something of delicate and unexpected beauty.

She had caught a few facts as she passed: that the Peace Crane was the best known model in origami. By reading a little more each day, she was building up her knowledge, in the same way that you added to the bird, with another fold. It was of intermediate difficulty, she read on Wednesday, but, on Thursday, if you followed the directions carefully, no problem: well worth it! On Friday, Step Three formed what would be known as the bird base. You folded the square on both diagonals, unfolded it flat each time, and turned the paper over. You then folded it in half and unfolded that, then folded it in half the other way, and left it folded. Fran remembered the Japanese girl. Very smiling and polite. She had made a menu for the canteen, describing all the healthy foods in a big banner of careful black calligraphy, that hung over the heads of jostling kids with plates of beans and chips, and pizza and chips, and cheeseburger and chips. There was a song, wasn't there, in South Pacific, where the handsome GI sang, "So far away, Philadelphia, Pee Ay…" and she wondered if the girl felt like this about Japan.

Fran never understood why these people suddenly appeared in school from other countries, and how they lived in lodgings with teachers or school governors. Did they cry into their pillows at night, and hate the staff-room and the cheeky children? How did they describe it when they got home? But she'd noticed, for all her doubts, an amazing thing. Just when you thought that the visitors would be at their most vulnerable, and the children most intractable, they suddenly came over all demure and attentive. It had happened with the Russian puppet lady, too. Nobody had been there to meet her from the Performing Arts' Department, so Fran had offered to go downstairs to the main door. The Russian woman had carried a bag full of rather dusty puppets that she'd made herself, and was going to give a talk about Pushkin, of all people. Fran knew this would be doomed, and when she looked in at the start, it was chaos, with the teacher-in-charge trying to settle the classes down – about fifty or sixty children, in a cold and dark hall, with poor acoustics.

The woman was introducing herself, and talking about Pushkin, and the children were spellbound, but not because she was fascinating. It was something cussed they just did, sometimes, as a kind of indulgence, to those adults who they instinctively knew would be of no use or relevance to their lives. They couldn't even understand her, because she spoke in a very thick accent about

Pushkin's life, and how he had stayed for his first six years, or something, in a basket, without speaking. Then she moved among the children with her hand up the back of an old peasant woman or a tired looking Cossack, saying, "Hello! You like me? Ha ar you today?"

On her way back to the main part of the school, Fran passed the origami display. There was something about a person called Sadako Sasaki, who had tried to fold a thousand cranes. She had lived in Hiroshima at the time of the atom bomb, and had had radiation sickness. Folding a thousand cranes was believed to bring good luck, it said, and good health, according to custom. Others had finished it for her, when she died, and a memorial had been erected in Hiroshima. Children from all over the world had sent chains of folded cranes to the memorial, to promote peace everywhere.

The Russian woman came up for coffee at break. No one seemed to be looking after her, so Fran made her a drink, and sat and talked to her. She was called Elena, and was a painter, as well as a puppet maker, she told her, and showed Fran a faded catalogue of her rather primitive paintings. She was in this country for a convention on Pushkin, she said. She talked about him as though he were an old friend, but no one else in the room showed any sign of having heard of him. There were deliberately banal conversations – an inversion of the children's appearance of being terrifically *au fait* with all things Russian.

Elena had henna-ed hair, and was about sixty. She looked like an old ballet teacher, and wore richly-coloured and textured materials – velvets and wool. She talked about the redemptive aspect of art, as the dolls' heads lolled from the carpet bag, and when the bell went, Fran took it upon herself to walk her to the main door, past the origami display.

Fran's best friend, Jules, also a teacher at a comprehensive school, was visiting at the weekend. She'd been good at origami at some point, Fran vaguely remembered. At their college lectures Fran had watched while Jules had flattened out bits of notepaper, before unidentifiable white shapes, purporting to be ducks or clowns, had littered their bench.

Fran told Jules about the Russian puppet lady.

"Yes, I know what you mean. I've taken the kids to exhibitions, and they've behaved well, just when you would expect it all to go wrong. One of mine is copying a Giacometti sculpture in matchsticks, would you believe! Her older sister was at our school – did some good things with art. She walks straight past me now with her pramload of infants– blanks me completely!" Jules sighed, her eyes still bright with her mission to transform and bring beauty to the lives of her pupils. Then she described how the younger girl had refused to get out of the classroom when requested to. "I told her to take her chair and sit in the corridor. She's bigger than me. Looks after the family now her sister's gone – no father; mother distracted, you know the score. She picked the chair up, and held it above her head and stood there for a moment as though she was going to bash me with it. Then she went out. Her probation officer's been in – the girl says I threatened her. And butter wouldn't melt, you know, in front of the head. But when I first showed her the Giacometti figures, she just took off – finding dead matchsticks in every nook and cranny on her way to school."

On Sunday, Fran waited with Jules on the platform for the train that would take her friend home, watching crisp packets flutter along the tracks, muffling herself up against the cold, her eyes watering a little as she squinted down the line. A woman with short, dirty bleached hair, pulled back into a ponytail with black roots, was smoking nearby. Fran observed the orange trademark stamped near the filtertip. The woman took a drag and all blurred into one – her mouth, the smoke, the dingy tints, her hair. The only clear thing about her was the beautiful grey eyes behind her glasses, exaggerated by the lens into great stark expanses of iris, pupil, eyelash and wrinkle. She was holding a pushchair with a little brown-skinned boy in it: he gave a velvety black glance from under his cap. While handing the child a bag of sweets, among which was a candy toothbrush, the woman spoke to Fran and Jules, through irregular teeth, stained with nicotine at the base. Lamely, the infant placed the brush in his mouth, then bit into the dull pink head, leaving a row of his own tiny toothmarks at which he gazed in wonder.

"Can I get a connection if I get off at Wootton? We're going to see me mate, aren't we, Jord?" She said she had moved out of the city: it was too violent. "Me fellah wants to go back. Nevah. There's kids torchin' cars ev'ry night. Nine years old. There's shootin'. A man was shot dead for eighty-five quid. There was a noise in me back kitchen one day and a bunch of kids had took me purse, emptied me freezah, and chucked all me meat and bread into the street. One pulled a chain out – me fellah's black – and said, 'We don't want no niggers here.' I told him to get out of me kitchen or I'd kill him." She picked Jordan's sweets off the bar of his chair, ate one absently and put the rest in her bag. The train was pulling in. "I don't want Jordan growing up there. He's coming back from his mam's swearin' and blindin' already. And he's only two."

"You must teach him it's wrong! Set an example!" Jules said, lifting the pram up. Fran frowned and tried to look both scandalised and serious, as she helped Jordan onto the train, obliquely glad that he would stay in the suburbs with his nan and his black grandpa. The train was full; the woman with Jordan stood in the passageway, and Jules sat opposite a mother with a little girl pressed into a corner, a baby on her lap, and a drowsing man next to her. Fran heard an announcement over the tannoy: there was a problem with the signals, and the train was not scheduled to leave for another ten minutes. Through the window, as though in suspended animation,

Fran saw plastic lego bits flying out from the infant's hand, hitting the man's sleeve jacket. The other child, taking out crayons, studiously flattened a sheet of paper on the table, her curls rich and full, the expression in her brown eyes happy, the urge in her to create, to be safe, to have pleasure. Eyes closed, the baby gripped a coloured plastic bottle, fingers settling instinctively into the right grooves. Then, asleep, she was placed on the seat beside the man, while her sister climbed onto her mother's knee, and shut her eyes. Her bare arms hung straight down at her sides, her body lay open and vulnerable, and her legs dangled down. Her mother sat back to read, oblivious to the involuntary jerks of her daughter's head. The baby frowned in her sleep, raising an arm which then fell heavily against the man's trousers. Fran reached up to the window spontaneously, to call the attention of the mother to the position of the arm. The square of paper lay forgotten on the table: neither bird nor beast. In Hiroshima city children like these and Jordan would have died of burns and leukaemia. An American airman on the plane – the Enola Gay? – that had dropped the bomb had said, "The city looked just like boiling tar beneath us," yet flying back all had been tranquil and smooth. Just following instructions. *So far away, Philadelphia, Pee Ay....*

Jordan's nan had manoeuvred herself into the seat next to Jules: Fran could see that the woman was smoking, despite the prohibition, with screwed up eyes, smiling politely as she listened to teacher. Jules's head bobbed happily as she talked: she would be entertaining her with some anecdote of school, no doubt, with all the enthusiasm of the Japanese exchange girl or Russian Elena.

She told Fran later that she had made an origami bird for Jordan, who had been bored. "I don't think he was especially interested – it wasn't really appropriate for a kid that age, but his nan liked it. She even had a go, and made a little boat."

If Jules had been there when the bomb had fallen upon

Hiroshima, she would not have allowed herself or those in her charge to accept that enormity without a strategy, however ill-conceived, for survival. She would have rounded survivors up, finding nicely-shaped bits of masonry, and shown them how to make mosaics with the broken bricks. Fran imagined Jules's practical, yet sensitive hands folding the paper in half on the train, explaining to Jordan's nan what you did next, helping her brown-stained fingers to press down the folds, acknowledging that it was hard, but, in the end, if you followed the instructions closely, it would all be worth it.

THE ARMIES OF THE NIGHT

Over time the Brompton *Argus* had seemed to lose its integrity, Mike explained to whomever was interested: "It had just become a matter of filling in around the ads. Not what I'd been working for at all." His section, he complained, had become a kind of production-line, with young subs who couldn't spell getting away with murder, and serious mistakes being made every week which no one had bothered to correct. His laborious, high-minded reviews had taken too him far long to compile, according to the snappish general editor, and no one could see what he was getting at anyway, half the time: his stuff was just "bloody affected". Mike had persevered in his battle for taste, while the front pages had become splashes of sensationalised rubbish, which the new reporters knocked out in ten minutes before heading for the pub.

He tried to forget the day it had all come apart for him. A new district reporter had gone home ill, and Mike had been assigned the lad's piece: it had been about a farmer who had neglected his lambs. They had been found starved to death in a field. Mike had spoken briefly to the man over the phone, then to the RSPCA. His story, alongside a photo of the lamb carcasses, had appeared next day under someone else's headline: "Carnage!" Later on in the morning the incensed farmer had stormed into the *Argus* editorial department, and had grabbed Mike by the throat.

"Keep your fucking nose out of my business, you fucking bastard."

The smell of the man's rancid breath was in Mike's nostrils as he approached Kingdom Hall: he saw again the bloodshot marble eyes; vividly aware of the splinters of straw on the dirty, torn tweed jacket sleeve. The farmer had borne down upon Mike like a mad bull: there had been copious spittle on his lips – *The buffoon was foaming at the mouth!* – and the other reporters had shifted away from the malodorous pig-shit spattered on the wellingtons.

In his terror, Mike had shouted to the receptionist to call the police. It had been a horribly embarrassing episode – *bestial*, as Ethel described it to friends – and Mike had totally over-reacted, as he had admitted to the amused constable and his furious editor, but his thing was, after all, as he had reminded everyone ironically later, beauty and truth.

Since that time Mike had been teaching people to write in Kingdom Hall. Mike had hated the place when he'd first started this one-morning-a-week job, because it reminded him too much of his boyhood. He'd grown up in this village, and Kingdom Hall had been where the Band of Hope had met. He'd got this job merely because of his work at the *Argus*, and a job was a job, as far as he was concerned, even if it was Mickey Mouse creative writing with the grown-up Band of Hope.

When he was eleven, Mike would walk past, on his way to or from his music lesson, treading on the little heaps of leaf dust and sycamore keys on the path through the park, hearing strident evangelical hymns, and stamping, or loud clapping, and the clash of tambourines and drums. The animalistic shouts of glee, the crude ardour seeping through the rickety slats, and the defiant vein to the raucous sound had made him shudder. In his mind it would always be associated with the council estate kids whose parents wanted them out of the way on Friday nights – kids like the hangers-about here, who despised and threatened the things he loved: pure and abstract things.

Mike, did, however, enjoy the lingering seasonal changes in the atmosphere on the walk along the Brompton seashore. In October, when the classes began, the track would be strewn for weeks with rocks hefted up by the autumn tides – the air crystalline with the sun making prisms of the salt spray filming his skin, at which he would smile and sniff, murmuring with pleasure odd lines from Arnold as he looked out over the gauzy ocean:

The sea is calm tonight
The tide is full, the moon lies fair
Upon the straits....

Kingdom Hall was a long wooden hut, with a faded greenish corrugated iron roof, where young out-of-work men played snooker and single mothers came to do their laundry, fill the urn with water for coffee, and then watch television, smoking and rocking babies in their prams. Every Thursday the caretaker would be waiting to lock up, on the dot, at noon, so Mike had to ensure that his class started stacking chairs and closing windows a few minutes early. Among Mike's present pupils was Francis, a nightclub compère from a neighbouring seaside resort, who wrote overblown tales about his mail-order bride; Lin, a divorcee and shoplifter, writing about her community service, and ex-alcoholic Bill, scribbling dislocated reams about his drunken exploits. What they thought they would attain, he would never know, he told Ethel over a sherry on Thursday evenings.

Mike had been swooped upon early in life by childless Aunt Ethel, who had been jilted by a philandering vicar and was constitutionally unable to find hope for nasty and brutish humankind. She sensed the child's finesse, she had explained bossily to his worn-out mum. He was destined for things of the mind. There was no possibility of anything lovely anymore, she said. Human beings were incontinent hogs. She would show him another way. Ethel had found poetry for him to read, and played him her long-playing scratched records of operas, wiping them with a yellow duster first. Mike, a creative and wan boy, had swiftly and easily renounced his mother and father, and moved into Ethel's nearby semi.

Passing a derelict entry that ran between the hall and the back of the boarded-up Milk Bar, Mike glanced along: among the scratchy brambles, a laughing teenager in a scoop-necked jumper and jeans was pulling herself free from the embrace of a lad.

Two young, fair lovers,
Fresh from the summer fields....

As she brushed past Mike, dragging the boy behind her, a cloying metallic smell from her sweaty hair and hot skin, too near to him, almost made him gag: he just caught sight of a purply-pink lovebite in the angle of her neck and shoulder. It occurred to him that he had never bestowed nor received a single one of these bruises, the badge of sexual allegiance and submission. Mike had known infatuation and desire, of course, like any man his age, but not for the life of him now could he imagine sucking blindly and lustfully, staining delicate female throats with those lurid blue-red weals. His school sweetheart, in fact, had dismissed him because of, he suspected, his reptilian lovemaking. Angela, though pretty, had been poor: always there had hung about her that same odour of his own rejected family – that of fetid corners, fags and frying. She had been precocious: at fifteen she had taken him into a field and instructed him, matter-of-factly, to deflower her. He remembered the cow-parsley in wide sprays behind her head: the white-pink pathos of his belly and thighs, and the rank and oozing Angela, so muscular and vital and predatory. As she had prepared herself, she had been telling him that she was going to start work in the laundry the following week. He would never go out to work, he'd replied: he was going to be a writer – he had realised early, with Ethel's help, that he was an aesthete.

"What will you write about? The fairies at the bottom of the garden?"

The girl had pushed him off her at the second or third vain attempt.

Stung, he had replied: "No, Angela. I'll be a literary critic."

"Same thing! Ponce who lives with his auntie!"

The memory of Angela's expression of loathing, her eyes squinting in the sun like mean darts, utterly constrained and depressed him, as the brazen evangelical music had, and as the newspaper office had. He had stood up in that field in his whiteness and pusillanimity, his trousers round his ankles, impudent flies buzzing towards the warmth and odour of his crotch. The drone of the insects had blurred with her light, sarcastic voice; he had been fixated by the swathes of silky, thick grass crushed under her elbow as she had leaned on them to speak; by the poignant beauty of the flashes of sunshine on her floral shift; the blonde hairs of her forearm gleaming like flax; the subtle freckling of her cheeks; the creamy mis-shapen front teeth; the thread of saliva swaying between her top and bottom molars as she opened her mouth to insult him. Mike had suddenly longed to escape Ethel; to be back with his family in the messy kitchen, eating chips and relaxing in his mother's affectionate glances and his dad's chirpy humour, but it was already too late: they had grown indifferent, hurt and confused by his rejection.

Already, at Kingdom Hall, there was someone sitting in the classroom. Ellen Moore, a young civil servant, had looked up when he entered with his briefcase, and was pushing a sheet of paper across the table towards him.

"It's a poem I'd like you to look at for me, before the others get here." Ellen's face was serene and he noticed the poise with which she sat back to wait. Unlocking the filing cabinet, Mike took out a folder of registers. He nodded at her – he would read and analyse her carefully-wrought, emotionally barren poem closely and honestly; they both knew that, because Ellen was articulate and serious about literature. Already she had enrolled on an Open University degree course and had discussed with him the modules she would follow. In conversation his heart had glowed when she alluded languidly to "devices" and "perspectives". A note informed Mike of the visit this morning of the moderator: the funders were sending in their quality assurance expert. As class members began to filter in and sit down, he told them not to worry if someone arrived to observe during the session.

"So we don't have to impress anyone? They won't be judging our writing?" Bill had already half-covered his short story with a document wallet. Lin blew her nose on a piece of straggling toilet tissue, then shoved it up her sleeve, before looking up at Mike in blank fear.

"Just be yourselves. It's me they're assessing, not you!"

They were nervous, nevertheless, and necks craned towards the window, amid small, apprehensive whispers, whenever a car drew up. Just as they were returning from their coffee break at the urn, a light knock came at the door. A woman looked around it in the sudden hush. She took her place at the table: she wore a cheesecloth dress, and a chiffon bandeau with trailing ends round her hair, and Mike saw the same rapt expressions on the faces of Francis, Bill and Lin as on Ethel's friends', when she held forth.

"Hello, everyone! I'm Barbara Lindsay – here to see if you're enjoying your classes and making progress. Many people have gone on to study full-time from Kingdom Hall!"

Mike weighed up his charges: Jack, the redundant china clay worker; Stella, the agoraphobic, who sometimes broke down in tears and left early; Jean, the dyslexic barmaid trying to write humorous magazine columns. He thanked his lucky stars for Ellen, continuing to breathe her rarefied air, ignorant of the fresh rush of alarm in the blood of her peers as they returned to the exercise they'd been working on. He passed Barbara a newspaper cutting.

"We're each writing a piece of autobiographical journalism to submit to the *Sunday Herald*, about people and events from our childhood."

Mike became aware of Francis's flashy plastic holdall; his surreptitious hair-combing; the vulgar bunch of keys at his tightly-belted middle and the bar of Aero in his pocket. He wished Bill didn't look and sound quite so much the recovering alcoholic, with his purply, open-pored nose. Lin, waiting to read her piece out, was like a schoolkid, biting her underlip and tearing on the worn-out tissue, leaving greyish crumbs on the cuffs of her shiny over-ironed jersey.

During the readings, Mike made his usual comments on grammar and clichés. Barbara, vaguely taking in the general ambience of AIDS wall posters and the groups of limbless clay figures from the pottery class, pleased by the career move from the library service which allowed her to wear these arty outfits, attended to Ellen's dainty piece on the Sunday School trips of her youth, with its perfect *mélange* of pastoral images.

"Right." Mike was up, shuffling papers together as he collected them in. "I'll send these in for you – get some personal details typed up and a passport pic by next time."

Mike had listened carefully as Jean described a photo of herself as a child, her nappy bulging out of too-big knitted orange knickers. There had been a line in Lin's story about a dying best friend, hair matted with vomit. A Jesuit priest had beaten a naked infant Bill with a rosary. Jack's miner father's moleskin frozen trousers had flapped in the wind all the way home. Stella's tale had been of the mother who would not hear of her daughter's abuse by her own father. Francis had written about his schizophrenic younger sister who had killed herself. In the end there was no escaping fags and chips, flies and fields, lovebites and shit and mad farmers: the reek and taint of existence insinuated from all sides, like the fucking armies of the fucking night.

The class moved off, as Barbara pushed through them towards Mike. Embarrassed by the syntactical howlers and sentimentality of the writing, he realised – shoving chairs on top of one another in a ridiculous pile which was sure to collapse – that he could not distinguish the real from the ideal, between life as it was and life as it could be, and since he was eleven, he had never been able to. He did not know what Barbara was looking for or what he was supposed to be doing with these people. They were almost illiterate, except for Ellen, who was plain pretentious. Mike saw that his judgement had disintegrated: he had lost all his confidence after the office, and after the farmer episode. Yet there was nothing in any of it to be afraid of, surely – rather to embrace, if he only dared.

Barbara was facing him, her eyes dull, as the class broke up. She was making a space for herself where she could deliver her verdict, ignoring his futile efforts to pile up the spiky-legged furniture before the caretaker got to them.

"I really enjoyed the session, Mike. Isn't it heartening that we've got a writer in the class?"

"You mean Ellen?"

The tower of chairs leaned precariously sideways: Mike was aware of interminable layers of chipped, moulded muddy-green plastic level with his face. Jean, Bill, Jack, Lin, Francis and Stella were back in their familiar world of flesh and rot and decay. He imagined the unwashed bottoms of single mums and snooker playing lads, and sensed the hardened balls of chewing gum and ancient bogies stuck on the seats' undersides. He wanted to cry: his arms ached as he tried to push the stack upright.

Barbara Lindsay was teasing out the edge of her bandeau, head to one side, viewing the wind-lifted tops of the sycamore beyond the car park. Her skin had a cold sheen, like fine paper.

"Yes. What's so nice is to find people who can distil base experience, and elevate it to a more *spiritual* plateau."

The door of Kingdom Hall banged shut, and a mother screamed at a kid to mind the road.

TINSEL

Between the varnished planks of wood on the pine bedroom floor glinted a thread of tinsel, drifted in from Christmas. It was now summer and the heavy horse chestnut she could see through the window wallowed dolefully in the air. One morning in the spring, Mrs Strang had opened her eyes to the hard, blue, brittle sky and to fresh leaves, spattered in lurid, luminous gobs on the branch. Like snot, she had thought, with surprise. She would never have been able to say that when Leonard had been alive. But that was the only word for it – it had that full, bursting richness: disturbing, insolent, incongruous, out of order, *punky*, iconoclastic... in the same way as fields of rapeseed. There you go, she said to herself – I've made snot romantic. What hope is there?

Straightening herself up in bed, Mrs Strang reached over for her pill bottles. Some little blue tablets she'd kept and they lay in their pack on the white lace doily: Leonard's tiny sedatives, polite reminders of him and his hypersensitivity. He'd hated it when his wife had friends round, and would retire early to bed with his eye-shades, grumbling about the chatter and laughter. But Esme Strang had cared for him throughout his long illness, until his dying day: life with Leonard had been all she had known for forty years. For six months now she had tried to work out a way of living and coping by herself, and the reality of that, and the sight of the blue pills, caused tears to well in her eyes.

Now she showered and dressed, slowly, pulling on her tights

with the gadget the social services people had given her. It opened and shut from a hinge, and was grey and ugly, like her walking stick: when she pointed at things with that, she felt insensitive and obstreperous, like the stereotypical old age pensioner.

Gradually, though, she thought, looking round the bedroom she had shared with her late husband, things were getting straight. She had a girl in to clean, even though she used a dishcloth for the paintwork on the staircase, and had never looked inside the oven to this day. But Esme had changed the pictures and bought a new, pink bedside lamp to replace Leonard's old anglepoise, and then had at last tackled the administrative stuff. To start, she had tried to understand what all the little pieces of paper that were stuck on a spike in the larder meant. There were receipts for television repairs, blurry blue-printed things about the Inland Revenue, curling-at-the-edges notifications from the Civil Service pensions' people, ancient hire purchase agreements and butcher's bills. They had made no sense at all to Esme, and without telling her friend, Olga, she had thrown the lot in the bin.

Olga had asked her last week what her plans were for the future, alone. Esme had looked round at the living-room, its sofa cushions in place still after her having tidied them up late at night, and pleased at the new order she had imposed, replied that she had none.

"Loneliness is a terrible thing, Esme. We don't want you going downhill."

Olga had sighed with the burden of the responsibility of friendship, and the diminishing pleasures of the life of the elderly. Esme had nodded, but had sensed an unexpected frisson at the same time. There was a shimmering *presentness* about everyday objects, that she couldn't explain. The grain of the wood on her kitchen table swirled in a pattern that seemed to pull her in, knives and forks nestled in rather a surreal manner in their drawer, and she had been caught off guard time and again by the shadow of a cloud passing across the lawn, or the mysterious manner in which her ornaments had become sculptural. She had picked up a pot funfair rabbit from a shelf, which Leonard had won for her in a shooting gallery when they were courting, and seen it as if for the first time, fixated by the lines of its ears, and the velvety, abstract curves of its haunches. Even the bits of paper on the spike had seemed to vibrate as she had pulled them off and spread them out to read; her "helping hand" had acquired a new grace – and then that particular green of the leaves outside, and the innocuous blue pills.

And the village where they lived seemed different, too: the streets became new to her; the wind whistled down from the sea, rattling eaves, and the cold air, harsh at the back of her throat, reminded her of stories and films from her youth, of Jack London tales, of the cruel north. Peeping through the pub window on a Saturday afternoon, she saw men crouching in the fug over copies of the *Sun*, and the football team arriving from their game by the wintry shore, all dripping hair and muddied legs and drenched green shirts with white collars, playing darts and guffawing. She had tried to put the sensation into words, for Olga. "It's raw here, isn't it – a man's world, like a trading post. I imagine blokes arriving with those tennis racquet things on their feet and piles of dead animals slung over their shoulders."

Olga worried even more, and asked the paper boy to let her know if Mrs Strang said anything out of the ordinary to him.

Leonard had not cared much about other people, or about the world, and, without considering it, Esme realised, she had absorbed this indifference. Yet now the trembling symbiosis of a fading silver moon at dawn and the white horses out at sea presented themselves to her subtly. With a shock, she studied the relationships between mothers and daughters, shopkeeper and customer, cat and sparrow.

Before she had married Leonard, Esme had enjoyed reading and walking, and conversation, and, in particular, had begun to be interested in philosophy and ways of seeing life. When she was young, she had wanted to find out about women pilots, and artists, and explorers, and writers and actresses. Leonard, in his reassuring tweeds and cavalry twills, with his pipe and his *Telegraph*, his politics and his military past, had represented something more tangible and substantial – he made her previous thinking seem frivolous and wayward. She had toed the line happily, because she could see no other line, and was incapable of drawing her own.

Now, she could. She could begin wherever she chose: she could keep a diary, and go to shows, and talk to the paper boy, Jeff, about his school and the teachers, and what he wanted to do when he left school.

"What did Mr Strang do?"

"He was a civil servant."

"Is that a good job, then?"

"I don't know. It paid the bills, I suppose, and meant we could go on holiday every year."

"Is that what you wanted?"

"I don't know."

He was conciliatory, as though she were a wayward child. "It's hard to know what you want to do, isn't it?" He looked into her face, and she saw where tea had left a stain at the corners of his mouth. "I think it's the hardest thing in the world. Because you have to decide on something that you think will make you happy, and it might not. But I suppose you can do anything now Mr Strang is dead, can't you?"

"But what if it doesn't make me happy?"

"Well, it won't really matter will it? It's now or never, and if you don't mind me saying so, Mrs Strang... you're, well, old."

He blushed at his own words, and picked up his bike to move off down the path. Mrs Strang's limbs became heavy, and she felt rooted to the doorstep, and she returned languidly to the kitchen

Tinsel

for her breakfast, the paper rolled up freshly in her hand, the scent of the newsprint strong and smudging her fingers.

Jeff had thought, as he listened to her, how Mrs Strang had talked about school, and asked him about music, and admired his new trainers. She was getting on a bit, and it wasn't that she was young at heart or anything corny like that, but there had been no motive behind what she said – she must be about sixty, but she was curious, interested in things for their own sake: she was a bit daft about things, like a kid. You could imagine her at Christmas, putting tinsel all over the house, just for the sake of it, because it shone and twinkled. He was sorry for her – that she hadn't seemed to have had much of a life – and decided he would never tell that interfering Mrs Micklethwaite about her behaviour, whatever she got up to, and rode off, lighter-hearted, to finish his round.

"Things have a rather beautiful, unreal quality since Leonard's death, you know," she confessed to her friend, over a cup of tea one afternoon. Once again, she had fallen into a kind of rapture as the steam from the drink wafted upwards, and the teaspoons lay crusting in the sugarbowl.

"Life's real enough. You're on your own too much. You need to get out and meet people – a Beetle Drive, say – find a new man, maybe."

Esme smiled at her friend, and shook her head. "I'm not looking for that kind of love, Olga. I'm enjoying life – for the first time. Is that a bad thing to say?"

There were buds of conkers on the big tree now, soaked in a warm light that lifted her heart. She would wash her pink sweater and rinse it in fabric conditioner, hang it out in this generous wind, then plant her irises and the many-coloured ixia and small hyacinths, in clusters. Her glance ran from the lowest boughs of the tree through a scintillation of gilded foliage up to the lazy motion of russet, easily-lifted topmost growth, mixing with the sky in a tawny, blue-gold fusion. A white butterfly was listing idiotically outside the window. It would be good to breathe the early-autumn air, skeined with cobwebs.

She lived through experience, watching it, and in her new notebook she began to record the signals of change she absently marvelled at: the piece of tinsel gleamed in the join of the floorboards, and a little spider ran up and down from the standard lamp, like a yo-yo, as she passed back and forth. Esme was mesmerised by texture, by colour, movement, storm and sunsets, falling fruit and opening flowers, clouds passing the window, the full glass on the bar and the then empty glass, the stars and the moon and the inky realms of heaven. She stared at and tried to register beauty and metamorphosis; she listened to and memorised inflections and vocabularies breathed on the air; the musical notes which hung and broke in her sitting room; watched the cat licking its white, submissive paw. The half-moon flew out of a white-blue morning sky like a crow from the horse chestnut tree, its leaves now thinning in a snow-gold litter, its shadowed trunk as silent as stone.

In later October days, she woke to the sight of the tree patched with bright flakes of heaven, its remaining verdure glowing in a dewy haze. The sunlit, lilting branches stirred giddily in the blustering wind, stilling themselves for balance before the next tirade, which teased and flummoxed in every corner – it was a chimera, a hurly-burly of bronze and flax, propellers and airsails, flags, beasts, flies, silks, goldfish, elves, cascading angels and dancers; a cadencing mess of endings, cold loops and spangles and spurting lucid forays, pinched rockets of quicksilver, hoots of night trains and greeny shiver of spindles, with the sky slinking down, around, between and beyond, in pale spites of blue.

There was a knock at the door: there stood Jeff, his bike leaning against the wall, the pathway strewn with small windfall apples. He dug in his pocket as she started to say she was just getting her tea ready.

"I'm going to be a deep-sea diver, I've decided. Or an astronomer. And you're not old; and I've got you a present."

He gave her a packet of Love Hearts. Then he was gone, and briefly the clouds blew past and covered the sun, and then a patch of light dawned on the slanting grass, which shone like shards of glass. Small branches of bramble bent slightly, and all the garden leaves shimmered and reflected light, from the shrubs, the bushes, the trees.

THE PRIVATE VIEW

I began to like New York, the racy, adventurous feel of it at night, and the satisfaction that the constant flicker of men and women and machines gives to the restless eye.
   F Scott Fitzgerald, *The Great Gatsby*

It's Rhyl, sometime in the eighties. Most of the electrical sign over Boots is missing. All that's visible now is the wiring, sticking out like antennae from the wall above where Morgan stands on the pavement. She has a couple of hours to kill before meeting her friends, so she'll have a drink and a meal. It's the inbetween time of day that Scott Fitzgerald describes in *The Great Gatsby*, but that's "racy, adventurous" New York, of course. Yet, like his narrator, in "the enchanted metropolitan twilight", Morgan feels a haunting loneliness – and a suspicion that she herself, like the young clerks he describes loitering in the dusk, might also be wasting the most poignant moments of night and life. In these wistful provincial streets are no joyous gangs of young sophisticates, nor singing voices nor the breathless charm of pell-mell theatre taxi rides. But Morgan senses beneath the melancholy veneer of the seaside resort in spring the same straining towards a vague, unnamed ideal, the same burning instinct for completion.

Afternoon is fading to evening, and she pauses a while longer, wondering if the pubs are open yet, then crosses the road and tries the door of The Lorne. Inside, a reddening sun shines through stained-glass windows, upon the bar and the too-early glasses of beer. A couple of labourers, tanned and tattooed, look at her as she enters, watch as she buys her beer and sits down, then pull chairs to surround her subtly. They put a record on the jukebox, parroting the words, "When will I see you again?" The phrases and sentiments are directed at Morgan simply because she's there and they're there; she's a woman and they're men, and there's nothing better to do. They drink more and play more songs: Morgan rises to leave; the sun is setting. A man in a suit follows her from the pub, and is watching her, as she halts in a glassy shop doorway, wondering where she can find somewhere to eat. As he lingers so obviously, she moves off, down the High Street towards the promenade, which she comes to as onto a prairie, in a sudden cold blast, where yellow sand is whisked along like seeds, yet fruitful and spiteful on her cheeks. The man is no longer behind her, and she is quite alone as she looks across the sea: its surface glints; the ocean is broad and tumultuous. The light, although still bright, illuminates only the undersides of the clouds and the folding waves: to Morgan, they seem monstrous, fungoid and exposed. She wonders if the summer sunshine, when it comes, will make a difference, and, aware of herself in the wind, fastening her belt and waiting, wonders what difference it makes if it's March or August, warm or cold.

She walks among the amusement arcades, open to the sea and sand, thinking about the labourers, and what they do in the dead of winter, and where their families are. Then she sees a toucan in a cage, emitting a reiterative recorded message from its red-enamelled bill. From the next alcove comes the refrain of a wooden Grandma Clampitt, rocking in her chair in the doorway, repeating hysterical wisdom to whoever puts money in the slot…then a faun, its moist, lacquered eyes reflecting only the angry movement of the clouds.

There are places to eat here, but something about the mute Chinese faces and the grubby menus depresses Morgan, and she takes a side-road into town, finding a place where she can sit and look out on the street. Opposite, a striped awning above a babies' clothes-shop bags and flaps. Morgan hears a fat lady nearby, speaking to the waitress: "I suppose you'll be glad when it's time to knock off?" She's shaking her newspaper exaggeratedly, sighing, mock-concerned, in a print frock and cardigan, wrapped up in an idea of herself that has no need of outside sanction.

"I don't really mind," the girl replies, deadpan, preoccupied with taking the order. "Hake and chips, and a small bottle of Hirondelle," the woman announces, then, bored, looks round and discovers Morgan. They're separated by an ornamental, wrought-iron railing, which partly obscures their view of one another, but the woman is undeterred.

"Where are you from? What are you doing in Rhyl?"

She neither looks at Morgan nor attends to the answers. There are further aimless conversational gambits that seem to serve purely to root the woman firmly in her own idiosyncratic domain.

"Haven't you seen a *chequebook* before?"

Morgan turns to see that the girl has now brought the bill, and the woman is flourishing a biro at her, red-cheeked and *quasi-*indignant.

As Morgan leaves, she sees the woman again outside the window. For a split second, she stands in shadow and wind, her flowered dress blown against her bulbous form, and, in that moment is not sure what to do next; there, in the world of expression and choice and free will, of hake and Hirondelle, there in the holiday resort at the start of the season, she cannot move. Morgan is appalled. Then life clicks into gear again, and the woman makes her decision, and walks down the road, as Morgan sits through the freshly piped, ersatz melodies of Golden Slumbers, How Much Is That Doggie, and Who Were You With Last Night?

It's time to meet her friends. She walks to the museum, where she finds the newly-built extension in pine and glass that houses the painting, craft and photography exhibition. The others are already there, and many strangers are clustered around the visiting celebrity. White and red wine is being dispensed from large decanters on long tables covered in heavy, damask cloths. Morgan walks through: she observes the layout of books and the subdued conversations, the hushed, appreciative murmur one comes across in the presence of Art, or the Great, or the Ineffable. She is told that the photographs have been taken in dangerous places by daring people, that the resident painter will be completing a mural in the library. She drinks one or two glasses of wine; she looks at the denim and wool and cotton and silk and leather of the private viewers: all is genuine, good and costly. The lighting is discreet, and the audience handsome to a man. There is no Grandma Clampitt, no loose wire, no flapping awning, no wrought iron, no chip papers, no labourers, no wind, no sun, no sea. Here is nostalgia, a longing for form: outside is chaos, rampant in the make-believe of the amusement arcade, in the parody of contact of the labourers and of the fat woman, in the fat woman's mad idea of herself. The balm of poignant moments filled with potential is absurd, as is the romantic desire – Gatsby's desire – to contain and possess: life pulses on randomly, terrifyingly. In the end nothing can harness or quantify the moment of hesitation, the desolation on the prom, the futility of the "season" when it comes, or the New York pause between daylight and dark.

She thinks of Gatsby, looking up "at an unfamiliar sky through frightening leaves", shivering at the rawness of sunlight and the grotesqueness of roses: his refusal to acknowledge reality, his arms held out wide to the dream, to the green light at the end of Daisy Buchanan's dock. *So we beat on, boats against the current....*

Under the night sky of Rhyl, Morgan turns for her train and for home, hearing the waves of the incoming tide against the sea-wall, in the dark.

THE SIAMESE TREE

The "pot" was not pot, but a red plastic tub, to which she took the large, unwieldy kitchen scissors at once. She ripped an inch down opposite sides, to try to fold them back somewhat, but the stuff proved unmalleable. Dirt spilled out in a light, black, free-for-all over the cream linoleum floor, making her pause. She took a newspaper, spread its two-page width, and tipped out the contents of the pot. As soon as the small tree was free, it was apparent that it was a conglomerate, a hotch-potch, a put-up Christmas job, a con, a fiddle, a wheeze: it was made up, intertwined only at its root system, of two puny stems of some nondescript fir. Bound together in the plastic pot it had looked like one plant, of course. Also, emanating from the soil and its mix of stones and hardened dogshit was the distinct smell of animal pee.

What a start to the festivities, she thought. But it might be OK, once it was fixed up. She dug about in her sack of decorations, feeling through the swathes of blue and green or silver tinsel for little carved rocking-horses, and red-hatted bandsmen, and painted bells. Faith was overwhelmed by the sensations she'd had at school, in her first Christmases: in the classroom, with the coal fire, and the smell of chalk, and the wooden partitions folded away for the Nativity play. All the children, from Standards Four and Five, would be cutting out stars, or making paper and silver trimmings. The teacher would be handing out coloured strips of tissue, pale blue and green and pink, showing them how to lick along one edge and stick it onto the other to make a loop, then thread another link through: soon there would be a room-long chain, stuck up with drawing pins. Best of all would be sitting with her friend Amy, and weaving the silver paper ones over each other, so they opened out to make a kind of geometric frieze. Lingering in her veins, in that rosy room, would be the illusion of the profound playfulness of her existence, and Faith would experience a stab of gratitude, and the sensation of freedom and privilege.

For ten or fifteen years now, the inseparable friends hadn't been in touch so frequently, although during their initial, manic episodes of divorce and subsequent inappropriate liaisons, they'd still had lots in common. Amy had scoffed at Faith's romanticism, and Faith had acknowledged Amy's pragmatism, and assumed that her friend would always be in her life: a fixture. Faith had moved away for a time, qualified late, failed to find a suitable partner, and written her books and poems, and Amy had stayed in their home town, working as a manager in a cut-price shop, taking annual coach holidays to Switzerland and Austria with a colleague. Occasionally, she had written to tell Faith about complicated intrigues with coach drivers, and, then, to Faith's surprise, had suddenly married one. By now, vast swathes of experience had passed unmarked, unlaughed-at and unexamined, and when Faith had playfully scolded her on the news of her wedding, Amy had seemed cross.

Despite these shifts and deteriorations, Faith knew the mutuality and peculiar wonder of their childhood could easily be retrieved by the odd phone call or birthday card. Or as last week, sympathy: Amy's sister Meg had died, after a short illness. Faith had half-expected this, after the first news of Meg's cancer, and although the occasion would be sad she was glad of the chance to see her friend again. Faith knew that they would soon be picking up the pieces, and laughing at their disastrous lives.

On top of the stove was a shining steel bowl that had been a free gift from a catalogue. Perfect. She scooped the soil into the bowl, pushed in the conjoined tree, without having disturbed it further at the root, watered it a little, which intensified the stink, and pressed the earth in with her hands. Presently the little tree stood proud in its silver bowl, and the plastic tub and the wet newspaper and the mess of soil was all thrown in the bin. Later, she took a dangling transparent tear-like pear, some stiff purple starry twine, a small red apple, a heavy gold star, a handful of silver lametta, and the lights, and before long the tree glowed in utter convention in Faith's living room.

Putting three satsumas in her pocket, deciding that the pretty indoor scene was worth the risk of fire, Faith opened the curtains so that others could see it, and set off on her walk, wondering about the interview yesterday. It wasn't that she thought the job should have been hers, but it had all ended so unsatisfactorily. She had been short-listed with another woman for some part-time English teaching, but neither had been appointed.

"If we find we need someone in the future, you're free to apply again, of course."

That would mean repeating the whole process, right from scratch, so they could forget it. She'd been there from eight-thirty to tea-time, and lunch at the canteen had cloaked her in the rank smell of chips for the interview. The presentation she had given – "on any topic of your choice" – was on imagery in writing. Twenty randomly selected neophytes, with pale, refusing faces had awaited her. Two interviewers had sat with notepads. She had asked the students what the word "imagery" meant. Nobody had answered.

"Look," Faith had said encouragingly, pointing to the word on the board, her hand blocking out the "ry" part.

"Pictures," one said.

"Yes!" she'd cried brightly, before proceeding with a sweeping claim for her special topic, the transforming power of the imagination, supported by hallucinatory examples from everyday speech.

"The bride *floated* down the aisle."

"His eyes were *coals*."

"I *flew* for the train."

Faith explained how the bride hadn't actually floated, but it was *as though* she had. Similarly, the man's eyes had not been actual coals, but had *looked* hard, and dense, and sparkled, perhaps. And "flying" for the train – it was obvious you couldn't do that, wasn't it?

The people with notepads had written away, and the girls at the back had giggled, and she had ended with a futile bet, since she was never to see them again, that they'd all have found an example of imagery before the day was over.

Almost a year ago Faith had decided to become a full-time writer: she had driven home from her job in her old car, to prepare for Christmas, quietly whooping for joy. She would have enough money to keep her going through the next year: the plan was to complete a novel, and earn her living entirely by writing. She'd expected, by now, to be living on a publisher's advance, but all she had, in fact, was many thousands of words, a pile of polite rejection slips, and one or two comments on the unusual or poetic quality of the prose. So, by the autumn, she had started to apply for work again.

The segments of fruit were cold, and she ate them two at a time as she wandered up past the golf course, trying not to look at the garage. She had asked the man to scrap her car in October, but there it stood, still, with its perfectly good tyres and cylinder head, and the complex automatic gear that screamed, which he'd said was too expensive to fix. The hill opposite was a rich pink in the setting sun, and the juice slipped down her throat as she reminded herself that it was no use agonising about it, the car was no longer hers and anyway she couldn't have afforded the equivalent of another month's bills, and another month's freedom to write. Her mind calmed as she moved on and heard golfers' voices on the frosty air.

"I'll see you in The Harp."

Then there was laughter and the slamming down of boot doors, and the end of the game, and the looking forward in their capsules of satisfied life to a pint at the end of the afternoon's sport. She envied these people she half-knew but never considered, wondering what they might be looking forward to at Christmas, and what they might feel about growing old.

Next morning, Faith put her black coat on for the funeral, noticing with interest that it was still lavishly speckled with bits of cotton from the cream-coloured linen interview scarf, crusting collar and cuffs as though with fine snow. At the crematorium, as Amy greeted relatives and friends, Faith was struck at once by the intensity of the stare in her old friend's eyes. In the cold, red brick building, Faith watched her, still responding to Amy's child-essence and the markers and memories of the past: the birth of siblings; the terraced house where the two would hide under the table from the parents and the tall uncles; the way they had scared themselves at Christmas, after school, going to the Co-op together to get Amy's family shopping, gigglingly frightened by the chimes of the village clock in the dusk, just as it might have sounded in *A Christmas Carol*, read to them by their teacher in those darkening afternoons. She remembered fondly the old docile collie dog, Prince, the infant Meg, the little brother, the manful lorry-driver dad, the smell of Lavenda polish, the cartoons in the *Daily Mirror*, and its blocky, blunt type whose huge claims to truth had made her feel oppressed and isolated.

After the funeral, they drove to a beach in Amy's battered car. She was telling Faith about Meg: "We had thought at first it was just ulcers." So when they'd gone for her sister's results, they had expected the same. "We were going to go shopping – just get the results and go."

But the consultant had asked if Meg knew why she was there, and there had been another doctor, too.

"'I've got ulcers, haven't I?' she said to him."

Then the consultant had said no, it was an inoperable tumour in her oesophagus, and there were four secondary lumps in her throat.

Amy had brought some pictures – photocopies of photographs, and some actual, glossy ones. In one from last Christmas, Meg was wearing reindeer horns, and looking down, mid-action, as she stepped onto a stool. She appeared perfectly well, better than Faith remembered her. Meg was born when they were nine and ten, and had always been there, vaguely, at the periphery of their lives. She gasped at how the young woman still looked as she had as a girl: the photographs brought back blurred memories of the youth of all of them as she studied the well-defined jaw and summer-tanned prettiness.

"Poor Meg."

"I feel guilty because I took my eye off the ball for a moment, and she died."

The bell of the lighthouse clanged dismally as they sat in the car. Amy looked like someone else, like the person Faith had seen in the crematorium. On her face there, silvery and blue, had been the terrified expression of unexpected age, and irrecoverable acts, of burden, responsibility, lost horizons. And it was here again, in a softer way, in her pallor, and the standing tears, and in the words of grief that hung like stones in the air, and the woody and blackened spirits of the pair rose ineluctably away from one another, as they gazed out at the hump of an island, and the distant mountains across the water.

WRITING TO JAKE SLINGER

Then this pure thing, vastly,
Consummately beautiful
Ten scarlet tulips, with sunlight
Blazing through to turn the red to gold
To make shadowing roses of their hectic
Inner bowls...

The first poem had been written: there hadn't been time to start painting, because I was having to catch the bus to go to work. This had irritated me, because I wanted to get my little book together. The idea was for a painting, a poem and a photograph of a few beautiful things, chosen at random. Perhaps an arbitrarily-chosen nook of the garden, I'd thought, to start with. This spontaneous shot would be the stimulus for the painting I would do – or "make", as I'd written to Jake in my letter (remembering just in time that artists *made* works of art: they didn't *do* them).

I'd already started looking around for something to photograph. I was going to do – make – a dozen or so poems, with paintings to illustrate them. I'd thought I'd like the original photograph, paper-clipped to the page of poetry, reproduced on one side, with the painting on the opposite. The photos would all be taken from an oblique, odd angle: the never-before-seen-in-this-day-and-this-light red tulips, a lilac bush, leaden with blossom, sycamore leaves dappling a stone wall, and some ill-defined twigs of a scraggy hawthorn bush, growing on a slanting field. In the poems, I'd try to forget the line that had gone before, and come untrammelled to each new thought. What I was after here was the beauty of chance association – what the Surrealists called *le merveilleux* in the everyday (that thing of the meeting on an operating table of a sewing machine and an umbrella).

Starting a painting now, though, would take too long: I would have to leave it till the evening, as the sun went down and the glass of red wine on the windowsill was no longer hectic in its bowl from its chasing of gold. I would drift into the small room I called my study, and stretch under the table for a string bag, from which I would tip my tubes of quick-drying acrylic paint. Then I'd take the dinner plate I used for a palette, with its edging of curling blue-green, like tendrils of sweet pea, almost obliterated by the thick gobbets of violet, magenta, cerulean blue at the rim, and, at the centre, impatiently-mixed reds, drying in a plastic film beneath the overlays of hot yellows I'd tried to reduce with ochres or cool umbers.

Anything, virtually, would do as a subject, I realised – when you looked, it was all chance configuration. There on the palette, even, was an Australia-shaped piece of Naples yellow, where a lake of lemon rested, spanned by a hair of dried paint that had spidered its way on the end of the brush to relocate itself in New South Wales: and there it lay in its frozen ceramic sea, flanked by basalt archipelagoes, and the flood-plains of a Communist land, angry red in this hectic bowl... well, plate.

The Surrealists wanted to undermine the authority of the museums, that separated works of art, and gave them "official" value. They were iconoclasts who believed in the irrational, in coincidence, memory, immediacy, desire, dreams, the hallucinatory....

Something had happened to me while I was looking so intently at the tulips. I must have concentrated too hard, because I swear I saw them moving with the sun – heliotropically – in the same way as I'd watched the sun itself fall down behind Anglesey the night before; that same sun, and now I saw the tulips moving in response to it. It was a kind of revelation – like seeing the grass grow – and I was a part of that mutable existence as I watched the flowers swerve and the sun give succour in its reeling passage through the spheres, and observed the breeze lift the blood red heads: all held as if in fine, dried webs of paint.

On the way to the bus, I bumped into a man I know: a bit of a piss-head, and stinking of alcohol now, but quite likeable, because rather larger than life. He had been shopping with his daughter, and she stood with the carrier bags while we said hello, her hair caught in springy plaits, her face blotched with freckles. He wore a tweed jacket and there was the sweet smell of booze and a warm, tangy atmosphere about them both as they stood in the sunshine on the path still strewn with the leaves of last autumn.

"I've been looking at some red tulips in my garden. I'm just stunned by them," I said.

"Ha! You'd better give them a kick, then," he remarked, in a rich baritone, heavy with beer.

I'd met Jake Slinger at the Tate, at the de Kooning show. We'd got on well, immediately, and it hadn't taken long for me to realise I was in the presence of a real aesthete. He was an art critic, he'd told me almost at once, reviewing the exhibition for a New York magazine. I'd asked him his opinion, eagerly, I know.

"It's incredible – and so awful to think that he has Alzheimer's and probably doesn't even realise it's on, or even what they sell for, or what an influence he's been." He proceeded, in the tea-room, with an acute and elegant analysis of international art trends, dipping sugar lumps into his black coffee as he talked. I'd watched the rapid osmotic flooding of the cube as the liquid passed through the granules, before he popped them into his mouth, one after the other. This geezer really knew his stuff, I thought: I was lucky to have made my overture in front of one of the "Woman" series. As we'd risen to leave, he'd given me his card, and I'd dropped him a self-conscious note to ask him what he thought of my project.

"If you're looking for it to be a commercial success, my advice would be to forget it – there's too much involved when you're using poems, photos and paintings. The best thing would be to bring it out as a fun thing. There's a girl I know at the Royal Academy who could suggest some publishers, but you'd have to fork out to fund it, I guess. Anyway, mention my name."

With his letter in my hand, I strolled into the garden. A breeze was blowing and the sun was still high in the sky. Of the ten tulips I'd written about, only one remained: wide, and wantonly open now, its style quite lost. It was surrounded by nine stalks, all topped by yellow-green knobs, which had been the centres of the blooms, leering blindly in the direction of the light. The fallen, heart-shaped red petals lay wilting in the leaves of maidenhair at their base. I knew this was timely, and that nourishment and growth continued in the plant, that the petals had served their purpose. But it was as though the tulips had been kicked.

TRUE LOVE WAYS

The light is good here on September mornings: everything gets a silver lift, even the edge of the bath ("Champagne? White? Avocado?" the builder had asked when he was doing the grant work. "Champagne, please!"). Having a bath on summer mornings isn't so great, because it's a dark little room, really. ("I love the shells, but it'll have to be white in here," said the letting agency woman Angie's called in. "With a light over the shaving mirror. And a towel rail.")

The shells Angie has painted on by hand, onto the red wall. They are yellow and indigo, with gold highlights on the round fat part of the body of the shell. They float down the red wall like ice-cream cornets. The sunshine picks out the halo and arm of the plaster Buddha, and the Christmas cracker ring it wears for a crown. It shines through a leaf of a trailing plant. It illuminates the edge of a lipstick, the lip of a bud vase that contains a white rose, and it fills the frosted window with pearl. Flickers of shadows – birds flying by – stain the sheen from time to time. Inside a small, conical piece of plastic on top of a cupboard, a cheap toy hare is suspended. When she'd left home her mother and father had taken up hobbies: Plasticraft was one. You collected dried flowers and leaves, or filched things from the mantelpiece and put them in these moulds, and then, she supposed, mixed the plastic up and it set and there were the little soldiers, buttercups, ferns, stars, etc, held timelessly, as if in aspic.

September was the time for getting your tights out, or stockings then, and going back to school and college, and making new friends, and shopping on Saturday in sweaters and jeans when you were fifteen, in 1958.

She phones her friend this morning, to let her know she is thinking of her. It is the anniversary of Lally's son's death: he drowned in a nearby river, when Lally was away. She remembers Lally, when she first came to art school, from London – she was a beatnik, and read *On The Road*, or at least had a copy in her bag. Others were as individual, consciously or unconsciously, with complicated Welsh names or old-fashioned outfits. In time, the girls who'd worn the elastic girdles had married the teachers, and those like Lally had got pregnant in the first few months. Angie remembers her anecdotes of lovemaking with the more eccentric painters in their midst, and the cottages where hundreds of empty, unwashed milk-bottles lined the windowsills and the back-yards. In this same September sunlight: spiteful and careless.

Lally has had, like other pregnant beatnik types, including Angie, a complex, messy marriage, and, unlike the rest, five more children. She doesn't paint any more. She seems glad of the phone call, telling Angie that her copy of the *Lady* hasn't arrived, and she needs it because there is a cheap cruise she wants to sign up for. Will Angie go with her?

"I can't. I might have to sell up or find some work or let or something. I've had to see the bank man about a loan. I'm skint."

Angie lies in the bath and looks at a mediocre watercolour of her own that she has nailed to the wall in front of her. Because of this ubiquitous light, even the tip of the panel pin gleams, in the slightly askew picture. The pin is fastened in the branches of a tree, and through the tree you can see the sea and the sand of the beach. She likes the winter because of this, because without leaves, through the trees, you can see the island and the beaches and the sunsets. In the summer, the whole is clouded over, if beauteously, with foliage.

A piece of cobalt sky in the picture jumps too far forward from the Indian red distant woodland. Here and there, where the brush has scumbled across the paper, paint has caught poetically, in layers. The picture almost works, but for that splodge of blue. But there is nothing to be done with watercolour. The painting brush paints, and having painted, moves on.

Lally was pregnant with a boy, who grew to be a man, and drowned in the river. None of the other brothers and a sister, Lally claims, can hold a candle to him.

When Angie had called this morning, she'd noticed music in the background in her friend's house, to her surprise on this sad day.

"Can you hear that, Ange? Buddy Holly. True Love Ways."

"Yes. I've always loved Buddy."

In school Angie had bought one or two of his records for her boyfriend, because Buddy was her favourite singer, and then at art college, in lodgings, she had heard True Love Ways for the first time, in the flat she shared with two other girls, over a grocer's shop, when she was in love for the first time in her life. The song was so innocent and tender, and she would lie on the sofa in the evenings, with the window open onto the street below, listening to it. On the mantelpiece had been postcards and prints of Vincent's Blue Nude, and others, Impressionists and Post-Impressionists – Bonnard's wife lying in the bath, and so on. They had thought they were in heaven, studying art, permitted ideas and attitudes that scandalised their parents: it was as though they flew inches above the earth each day.

Today Angie is going to see someone at the Job Centre, about a thing called the New Deal. If you were over fifty and started work, and earned below a certain amount, the government topped it up, or something. Her father had worked for these people when it was the National Assistance Board, and she has always felt she should have a special dispensation, but of course no one remembers him now, and she herself can't really believe that she is signing on, or whatever the term is. "Everyone imagined themselves privileged, exempt. Even an ugly old crone watering a geranium on her front porch" – she reads Charles Bukowski's *Women* at the bus stop. By an elderberry bush she watches a wasp creeping over a white ball on a tree: a snowball plant, maybe, and five elderberries gleam in the golden sunshine of mid-day.

On the bus a young man with tousled curls and a beard reads a huge book – she sees it is called *Titan* or *Titanic*, maybe: behind him an older man in a tweed hat looks up anxiously as a baby cries. The mother rocks the child, but still it screams in the sunlight. The women on the bus glance across sympathetically; the infant's leg jerks back and forth compulsively: it has wind, the women all think. The men are uninvolved, despite a wedding ring on the finger of the bearded one with the book, and the cleanly-washed lightweight blouson jacket of the second. A slightly rancid odour wafts from two women in front – a mix of cigarettes and deodorant and unwashed hair, given off when they move in the warmth of the sun, from their sitting positions, to raise an arm or steady themselves on the shining rail. Finally, the baby's mother gets up to fetch a primrose-coloured cloth from her bag, stashed in the railed-off section near the front, and drapes the child's head and shoulders in it, and it is quiet, its little hand stretching up and over the cheek of its mother, and she kisses its fingers absently, while gazing at the fields and trees of early September, and the stretched white cloud across the paling cerulean blue. That is the blue she should have used in the watercolour in the bathroom, Angie decides, as the shadow of her head shifts across the back of the seat, and the bus turns a corner onto the road into town.

In the Job Centre a woman called Marian Jones is ready for Angie. She guides her up the stairs to her office.

"I like your shoes," she says from below Marian. They are black, high-heeled, suede, strappy.

Marian does not flinch as she opens the door. "It's very hot in here, I'm afraid." She fishes around in the file cupboard and brings out a wad of papers to be signed. Angie has to show her the business plan that the bank has approved. Marian Jones frowns and picks up the phone and says that she might just have to run it past her bosses in Newcastle. "We have a clause about writers and artists."

The people in Newcastle say they will call back with their verdict. Marian Jones seems scared of the bosses, but she knows the paragraph, section so-and-so, that forbids giving money to writers and artists, alright.

"But it's advertising features – that's what I'll be doing. It isn't the same."

In the way that reading the *Lady* isn't being a painter. Lally had been good: her sketchbook full of small gouaches in vivid yellow and blacks, and she had walked round with Beat writings in her bag, and had got pregnant.

Marian Jones looks pleased when someone rings back and says it's OK: "If the bank has approved it, we can't very well say no, can we?" she repeats to Angie, relishing the verbatim report, and charmingly excited at having won through, while toeing the line of section such-and-such, paragraph so-and-so, in her daring suede high-heels.

Angie thanks Marian. "Good job I complimented you on the shoes!"

Marian Jones is in conflict suddenly; a stranger to irony and flattery from a woman; stricken to her root with the question of her identity; unsure of the importance of the bosses in Newcastle, and her Dorothy Perkins' top and the hot office and the kind assistance she has just given.

The afternoon billows forth in the dust as Angie leaves the building to catch the train home. She stands on the platform looking out to sea. Someone has a transistor radio on, broadcasting an arts programme – she hears part of a conversation about John Constable.

"His wife was consumptive, and he got her pregnant eight times in fairly rapid succession."

"That's how it was then. He was the one with the talent, after all."

Angie turns to the sea and catches the final comment.

"But she died so young!"

From the waves, a dark shape lurches out and back: heavy and sleek. She thinks it might be a dolphin – they have been known to appear here. Then there is another, and two more, with the filmy sun catching their brilliant white undersides. She turns to tell someone, and there is no one there, so she watches in solitude. Then a man arrives with his bike, and she describes what she has seen.

"It'll be dolphins, yes – they've been talking about them at work this week."

He is a nature warden and he has a little telescope in his bag, which he digs out and shows her how to use. She scans the blurred horizon, and sees the black shapes, further away now, but certainly in a group. He talks to her about his job and his family. They have fun with the kids, because his wife is Swedish, and they can make jokes in Swedish and English and Welsh. He doesn't earn much money, and neither of them is very materialistic, he says. "Or worldly-wise." He is bothered when friends of the children call; by the way they dress and talk.

"They'll be wanting trainers and so on, soon," she suggests.

"My wife gets a lot of clothes from charity shops – football shirts and stuff."

"But you won't always be able to fob charity things off on them. Peer group pressure, and all that."

He frowns and reluctantly acknowledges it. She envies his innocence and the concern he has for his wife and children. He wants to stay in the world of countryside care, bikes and sandwich tins, Oxfam, family life, puns in every language, and true love ways.

"Maybe she could find work. She has a degree in psychology. Maybe she could get a job to fit in with school," he offers.

"In a supermarket, you mean?"

"P'raps. Or a doctor's. Be a receptionist."

The dolphins have gone altogether.

The sun's rays slant across the mountains and the open sea, catching the underside of a jet trail and burnishing it, as it evaporates in broadening, silent, weakening flakes of cloud over the bright, deceiving water.

THE NET

They were all sitting on this crag or outcrop thing: all were casting sidelong glances when they believed they were not being observed; all wishing they had worn the other jacket or dress; all feeling wrong about themselves; that everyone else was right.

Among the group was the groom's father, a rather swarthy, intense man, lean, in blue linen jacket and light trousers. The night before, he had watched the moon come up over the water, from the beach where he was camping with his daughter.

"We'll have to let them know we might not make it: it depends on the tide, tell them. Say we're camping on Pebble Island."

"Text or phone?" She was glad to be on her own with her dad: she wished her parents had stayed together; she dreaded, in a way, the day ahead. It would be good if they actually were unable to go, but she guessed this was just an infantile desire for her own psychological safety.

"Either. I don't understand these things."

The waves lapped the shore. She put her toes in: it was perfect. The water was clear but viscous, warm, with the shells and stones underneath showing through in a soothing, harmonious blend of brown and cream, black, white, pink and gold. Smaller stones, almost sand, trickled and sifted across mussel shells with the motion of the sea.

"The mills of God grind slow, but they grind exceeding small," she said contentedly. She liked "exceeding", rather than

The Net

"exceedingly": it seemed more final and uncompromising. She liked the sentiment, too: in the end, you didn't get away with anything – what went round, came round. So she'd better put a block on the resentment in her heart, and swim, if she had to, to get to the wedding.

But of course, it had been OK. They had packed up methodically, and all the bags were zipped up and thrown into the boot. The father's jacket swung from a coat hanger inside the back door; with the boot open the sun caught its slightly crumpled blue sleeve. She thought how irritating it looked in the midst of tent poles and plastic water bottles: a reminder of duty and real life.

"I hate coat hangers, Dad. They make you look like a travelling salesman."

He did not relish getting out of his shorts and vest into the ceremonial garb, and his heart sank a little, too. He had enjoyed this simple interlude under the stars. Across the water, his ex-wife Carol asked the bride's mother for a go of her lipstick.

"Pink, if you have it. Red turns me into a vamp."

The bride's aunt started to say something about herself and red versus pink lipstick. She was also trying her glasses on under her yellow hat in the mirror.

"I feel as though I've got too many things going on around my face. I might read without my specs," she was saying.

The bride's mother, Stella, was telling her that the specs looked good: Carol, the groom's mother, applying Cute Pink, felt she had probably always tried to make people feel good about themselves. She wondered if Stella might find this effort trying, ever.

The aunt placed her glasses back in their case, and snapped it shut. Outside in the broad panelled hallway, guests stood about, wondering whether they should sit in the room where the service would be held, or go outside to welcome the bride. Carol thought it would be nice to go and see how she looked: her daughter-in-law-to-be.

The Net

They had been arguing, weeks earlier, about money. Carol had wanted Inez, the daughter-in-law-to-be, to stop interfering in her relationship with her son, the groom, Ralph. Carol and Ralph had always been close. Ralph had helped Carol financially and now Inez was putting her foot down. Carol had accused Inez of coming between herself and Ralph. That's what brides do, though, she supposed, listening to the sound of her own heels on the wooden floor as she set off towards the main door. Outside in the sun she was startled to see Inez with her dad, Boyo. Carol had never asked his real name, and Boyo suited him, anyway. She didn't like him, but had to admit he had charisma. Boyo was paying for most of this, including the cost of Inez's smooth satin dress, which hung in folds like milk, cascading across the rough stone steps where she posed for pictures. Inez, Boyo and one or two bridesmaids stood smiling, seemingly at Carol herself, in the sunshine. Passers-by stood to look at the colours and fabrics, the hats and flowers, the ritual and display, the refusals and hopes. In T-shirts and floppy hats, with guidebooks and haversacks, they milled past and stared, with reddened arms, taking off and putting on sunglasses, picking up and putting down infants, safe in the world of after-the-event, their thoughts of Monday morning and the ironing, or the mistress, or the bank, or the window-cleaner, or the cancer specialist, or the central heating boiler.

Carol noticed how the painted blue walls of a tower blazed in the sunshine. Then the small bridal party began moving forward, and the air was displaced as skirts and baskets of posies were re-arranged around the principal players. The wedding was being filmed, and the photographer manoueuvred himself through the watching groups, holding his camera with one hand over their heads, keeping his focus on Inez and Boyo.

Carol slipped into the moving party and they passed as one, up the steps into the corridor once more, and through to the room where the ceremony would be conducted. She saw that her ex-husband, Damien, and her middle daughter, Toots, had arrived from the absurd money-saving overnight camping: Damien was taking pains not to be close to Carol, as they were placed in their seats by the bride's mother. A man in a velvet suit would be the witness, and the aunt in yellow would read a poem.

The front rows were filling up with Inez's family and friends, Carol's other daughters, and Boyo and his new wife. The registrar, a woman, stood in a dull checked blouse and black trousers and explained the procedure to the assembly with a bright, accustomed smile. No one knew of any reason why the marriage should not take place, so the bride and groom were able to plight their troth, which they did, falteringly but happily. Carol felt a hot arm next to hers, and her eyes brimmed with tears, and she did not dare look round. The aunt was now reading a Christina Rossetti poem, and her voice had become emotional. Carol heard the words "peacocks", and "pomegranates" and "silver fleurs-de-lys" and wondered what "vair" meant. She noticed that the aunt's lipstick had settled somewhere between pink and red, luckily matching the nail varnish on the trembling fingers holding the piece of embossed card upon which the poem was mounted. A small gold angel with a trumpet floated down and onto the floor: Carol imagined the aunt had pasted it onto the poem as decoration, and used a paper glue, such as Prittstick. A harpist resumed some unrecognisable, discreet background airs, as the register was signed. People were now beginning to look for things to throw; Stella dipped into a box and the aunt gave out handfuls of rose petals from a long, narrow paper bag, stiff with motifs of bells and bows.

"Here," she was saying, as she pressed dried petals upon guests, "they're from my garden. I've been drying them for months on a tray in the kitchen."

She didn't say that the cat had sometimes curled up on them in the sun, and that she'd had to shake out the gleaming hairs before filling her bag. The petals' colours had now faded from what had been brilliant soft reds and warm yellows and white, to browns and beiges and faded carmines, like the skin of an old woman.

"They smell lovely!" someone said.

Stella confessed smilingly to Carol that she had squirted her own bought boxful of petals with rose oil, and the aunt looked briefly dismayed that the perfume was not from those she had collected over so many weeks. Someone in the crowd was replying to a question about a recent bout of depression: "It's a matter of getting used to the desperate trap that is oneself."

The sky remained cloudless; the blue wall vibrated in the heat, and Boyo suddenly remembered that tomorrow would be the anniversary of his own marriage to Stella. His new wife, Freda, was guiding people towards the restaurant: he wondered if he should mention the fact, and decided against it. She was an unsentimental woman, but who knew what her perception of this recollection would be?

The aunt, he noticed, was glancing back at the swathe of rose petals across the cobbles, then turned with a vague, unfocused smile to join the stragglers. He hadn't seen her for years now, and she had barely spoken, still burning with anger at him for his betrayal of her sister. The petals on the cobbles reminded him of a day when he and Stella had met by accident in the street in spring, a week before the divorce. She had been looking in a shop window at bird cages when he had caught up with her. Because no one could see them and they felt momentarily freed from the context of blame and recrimination, they had fallen into the conversations of old: the kind of bird that would be best for a conservatory; whether the stand would suit; was it rather too ornate, and so on.

"I'm going for a pie to Evans's, through the churchyard. Do you want to walk along?" She had strolled with him to the grocer's, past the gravestones in the grass. The pork pies had all gone, so he had settled on a steak and Stilton. "I want *beercan*, too," he had said, and, puzzled, she had waited while the pie was wrapped.

"You can't get beer here."

"No – *beercan*. Bacon! It's what Freda's lad calls it. And half a dozen organic eggs."

She had said goodbye outside the shop, and he'd watched her walk along the cobbled street, and round the corner, and out of sight, before turning for his new home, his steak and Stilton pie warm in its paper bag in his hand. Stella would be wondering when he had started to eat meat, he knew, and had been too polite or feigned too little interest to ask. Like the idea of caged birds, it was too big an issue: too redolent of their own pledges to one another on vegetarianism, liberal politics and all the rest.

Someone was calling people to the table, where they sat at their places, where little cards with their names inscribed lay. Ralph made a speech, thanking Boyo and Freda, then Inez cut into the blue iced cake that her mother had made. Freda refused her piece; Damien leaned back in his chair in his blue linen jacket, hoping he'd packed the fishing tackle and the camping things properly. Carol, lipstick-free, saw that Damien's shirt could have done with a once-over with the iron. She babbled about the sixties to a bridesmaid, and called for more champagne. Boyo stood and awkwardly welcomed his new son-in-law into his life.

Later, the guests sat squinting in the garden, drinking Pimms and strolling near the seashore. A party that included the bride took a path through marram grass towards the beach. The rocks were wet, glistening in the evening light. Across the smooth water lay fields and dense woods, settled and calm, as though many summer evenings such as this had passed. The bride's dress seemed molten in the heat and light, as she twirled and posed for more pictures on the sand. Where her hem had trailed, it was black, splashed and ruined in a second. Yet she gathered the skirts in her arms, stains and all, as people reminded her that it was only once, that she'd never wear it again. She seemed for a moment perversely intent on divesting her dress of its glamour and power, and stepped with a laugh into the estuary mud at the water's edge.

The group was gathering higher up in the still strong sunlight, sitting with cigarettes and passing round a bottle of champagne, at last discovering whose relationship was to whom. Damien's blue jacket set off his deep tan, and his brown eyes flashed as he introduced himself properly to the aunt, who tried to reconcile the stories she had heard, of violent quarrels on another continent. In her dusty pink sandals Carol talked to Stella. Younger wives passed babies between them, or held them on their hips as though they had always been mothers. Their husbands, with stylish hair and studied casualness, joked and laughed, forming new friendships and indifferences. In the distance was the building where the wedding had been: its blocks of colour still vibrant against the fields and woodland. Estuary birds flew out in small flocks at the voices from the crag. Water lapped the shore, shifting shells and drifts of seaweed.

The bride at last relaxed and embraced her new husband, like the old friend he once had been. A new wave was forming over the strands of what had been a fishing net, lost or discarded years ago. The net lifted slightly with the swell, then was moved forward a little, and then fell back once more.